L'AMANTE ANGLAISE

L'AMANTE ANGLAISE

Marguerite Duras

Translated from the French
by Barbara Bray

PANTHEON BOOKS NEW YORK

For Jean Schuster

First American Paperback Edition

Library of Congress Cataloging-in-Publication Data

Duras, Marguerite.
L'amante anglaise.

Translation of: L'amante anglaise.
I. Title.
PQ2607.U8245A6313   1987   843'.912   86-25286
ISBN 0-394-75022-5

Manufactured in the United States of America

I

— Everything that's said here is recorded. A book is starting to come into existence about the crime at Viorne. You've agreed to describe what happened in the café Balto on the evening of April 13.
— Yes.
— I have here a copy of the recording that was made there that evening without your knowledge. It gives an exact rendering of all that was said, but it just repeats the words blindly, opaquely. So it's up to you to set the book in motion. And when what you've said has given that evening back its real depth and dimensions we can let the tape recite what it remembers and the reader can take your place.
— How about the difference between what I know and what I say — what will you do about that?
— That's the part of the book the reader has to supply for himself. It exists in any book.

Would you mind introducing yourself?
— My name's Robert Lamy. I'm forty-seven. I took over the Balto at Viorne eight years ago.
— Before the evening of April 13 you didn't know any more about the crime than anybody else in Viorne?
— No. I just knew what it said in the announcement.
— Try to speak as if there hadn't been any newspapers since the evening of April 13.
— What if I can't always manage to forget what I know now?
— Say so at the time.
So that the reader is in the same position with regard to the crime as you were on the evening of April 13, we'll

begin by re-recording the public announcement issued by the Viorne police, which at the beginning of the evening in question had just been read out for the third time that day.

"As has already been made known in the press, various human remains have recently been discovered in goods trucks in different parts of France.

"Police pathologists have come to the conclusion that all these remains belong to the same body. With the exception of the head, which has not been found, a reconstruction of the body has been made in Paris.

"Analysis of the railway intersections shows that all the trains concerned, whatever their destination, passed through the same point, i.e. the viaduct at Viorne. Since the remains must therefore have been thrown down on to the trucks from the parapet of that viaduct, it is probable that the crime itself was committed in this commune.

"The town council accordingly urges local residents to do all in their power to help the police clear up the matter as soon as possible.

"If anyone knows of any missing person of the female sex, of medium height and stocky build, between the ages of thirty-five and forty, will they please notify the police at once."

— Well, of course I knew Claire and Pierre Lannes, and Alfonso Rignieri. They were among the fifty or so people who were my regular customers. I also knew Marie-Thérèse Bousquet, their cousin. She used to come to the café sometimes with Pierre and Claire just before dinner, or late at night with the Portuguese workers. Of course I didn't know her so well as I knew the others: she was deaf and dumb, and that sort of restricted contact.

Pierre and Claire Lannes used to come to my place practically every evening after dinner, between eight and

4

nine. But sometimes they wouldn't come for several days running, not necessarily because one of them was ill, but because they didn't feel like going out, or they were feeling low, or tired.

I'd got into the habit of not asking Pierre why I hadn't seen them the previous day or the last few evenings. Tact. I'd noticed — or so I thought — that he didn't like being asked how he'd been and what he'd been doing. Matter of delicacy, I think.

So when he came in on April 13 I didn't ask him why he hadn't been in for five days.

It was eight o'clock in the evening.

They'd just read the police announcement out for the third time that day, out there in the square. I was laughing over that bit about analysis of the intersections. I was just telling Alfonso I couldn't help laughing when Pierre came in. He was alone. He quite often used to come in without Claire—drop straight in on his way home from the office. We said hallo, and I asked him right away whether he'd have thought of the catch about the intersections. He said he wasn't sure.

I thought he looked tired and not so well turned out as usual—he was always very spick and span. He had a blue shirt on and the collar was a bit grubby. I remember noticing, saying to myself I wonder what's wrong.

Not many people had been into the Balto in the evening since the murder.

There were five of us that evening: Alfonso, Pierre, a man and a girl nobody had seen before, and me. The man was reading a paper. He'd got a big black brief-case on the floor beside him. We had a good look at him, the three of us. He looked exactly like a plain-clothes detective but we couldn't be sure because of the girl with him. He didn't seem to be listening to us. She was — she'd even laughed when I mentioned the intersections.

5

But as neither Alfonso nor Pierre seemed inclined to share the joke I didn't say any more about the intersections.

It was Pierre that started the conversation off about the murder again. He asked me if I thought it would be possible to identify the victim, in view of the fact that they couldn't find the head. I said it'd probably be difficult but still possible — there were still birth-marks, irregularities, scars and so on: everybody's body was different from everybody else's.

There was a long silence. In spite of himself everyone was trying to think which woman in Viorne could correspond to the description of the victim.

It was during the silence that I first noticed Claire's absence.

I mean it was then that her absence suddenly struck me, and that I connected her not being there with Pierre's looking worried. I didn't ask him about her, but it did just occur to me that perhaps it wouldn't be long now before he'd have to leave her. It was Alfonso who asked after her, just as if he'd guessed what I was thinking. "Claire's not ill, is she?" And Pierre said: "She'll be along — she had something to do in the house. No, she's not ill, just tired." Very tired, he said; but it was probably nothing serious — perhaps just the spring.

Then the conversation went on again, still about the murder.

I remember I was getting worked up about the savage way the murderer had dismembered the body, when Alfonso said something that surprised us. He said: "Perhaps it was just that the body was too heavy to carry in one piece, and there was no alternative." Pierre and I hadn't thought of that. Then Pierre said those three nights must have seemed endless to the murderer. Then the girl spoke. She pointed out that during those three nights the murderer must have made nine trips to the viaduct, ten if you counted the head. She said the business about the intersections was the talk of Paris. We got into conversation with her. I asked her what else they were saying in Paris. She said people thought it was a madman who'd done it — one more nut from Seine-et-Oise.

Then Claire came in.

She was wearing the navy-blue mac she used to put on when it rained. It was a fine evening. In one hand she was carrying a little case and in the other she'd got a black oilcloth shopping-bag.

She saw the strangers and went straight over to Alfonso. Everyone said good-evening, and she answered. But I could see she wasn't pleased that there were strangers. I heard a newspaper rustle and saw that the man had stopped reading and was looking at her. I just noticed it, that's all. Claire's manner didn't surprise us any more, but it might attract the attention of someone who didn't know her.

— *What sort of manner?*

— Grim.

Pierre suddenly started towards her as if to conceal her. He pointed to the case. What was that for? She said: "I'm going to Cahors." Pierre restrained himself, forced a smile, and said so that everyone could hear: "I was just thinking of taking a few days off and suggesting we go."

No one believed him.

She didn't answer. She stood there nonplussed for a minute or so, then went and sat down by Alfonso at a table on its own.

It was as I went over to serve her that I remembered all three of them came from Cahors, but in all the eight years I'd known them they hadn't been back. I asked her: "How long are you going for?" She said: "Five days." Then I asked: "When did you last go back?" She said: "Never." Then immediately after that she asked what we were talking about before she came, whether it was about the murder, and if so what we were saying about it. Alfonso told her yes we were talking about the murder, but we weren't saying anything important. She seemed even more withdrawn than usual. I thought it was because there were strangers present.

— *How did she look? Sad? Tired?*

— No, I wouldn't say that.

We went on talking about the murder, of course — the number of trains that go under the viaduct every night, the number of journeys the murderer made — and suddenly she turned to Alfonso and asked him: "And didn't anybody see anyone at night near the viaduct?" Alfonso answered: "Nobody's gone and said so, at any rate." When he said that Pierre turned and stared at him. Then he said: "Didn't *you* see anyone near the viaduct at night, Alfonso?"

Alfonso shrugged his shoulders impatiently and said no, don't keep on.

From that moment a sort of constraint descended on everybody, I was sure I wasn't imagining it. Pierre's and Claire's anxiety to find out whether Alfonso had met the murderer made everyone feel uneasy, especially in front of that man.

In spite of the constraint we went on talking about the murder.

We talked about the police's house-to-house visits to the local inhabitants. They'd been to Alfonso's the night before and to my place that same morning.

Claire wanted to know what questions they asked. I told her they asked people for their identity papers and to account for the absence of any member of the household who wasn't there.

Alfonso said a team with police-dogs had been searching for the head since the morning. Claire said: "Where?" and Alfonso said: "In the forest."

After that I don't think she said anything for some time.

The men went on talking about the murder. How long exactly I don't know. Perhaps half an hour. Suddenly when you looked out into the square it was dark.

I told them the police had asked me to keep the café open. I said it seemed funny having a café open till midnight in a godforsaken hole like Viorne. The girl asked why the police wanted me to stay open. I said: "Because of the old law that a murderer always returns to the scene of the crime." "In that case all we have to do is wait," said the girl.

That was the sort of thing.

Oh yes, at one point Claire and Alfonso said something to one another — not much, just a couple of sentences. I caught the words "fear in Viorne" — that was Alfonso. He smiled.

Another time the girl went over to Claire and asked her: "But what about your train, madame?" Claire gave a start and said: "What train?" Then she pulled herself together and said that the train for Cahors — I remember this perfectly — left the Gare d'Austerlitz at 7.13 in the morning.

The girl laughed. We forced a laugh too.

The girl said Claire certainly left herself plenty of time. Claire didn't answer. The girl asked whether Cahors was a nice place. Claire still didn't answer.

The constraint was getting more and more oppressive. We racked our brains for something to say.

And then suddenly the man stood up. He strolled over to the bar as friendly as you please and wanted to know if he could stand a round. I made some nasty remark, like:

9

If you think you'll get anything out of us you're wasting your time and your money. Naturally he didn't take any notice.

We drank. I wanted to find out whether he really was from the police. I said: "And do the lady and gentleman come from Seine-et-Oise?" The girl said she was from Paris — she'd come to have a look at the scene of the crime and the gentleman had asked her to have a drink. He smiled and made a pun that didn't make anybody laugh. He said: "No, I'm from the Seine."*

So then we knew exactly who we had to deal with. And yet no one left. Everyone stayed there, waiting. Presumably waiting for him to tell us something about the murder.

— *Didn't Claire say anything?*

— Oh yes. She didn't understand what the man had meant. She asked Pierre: "What was that he said?" and he answered very quietly — but I heard, and the detective must have done too, you could have heard a pin drop: "He's a cop."

So we knew. It turned us all up. But nobody left. Everyone stayed, and waited.

Where was I?

— *The detective was offering you all a drink.*

— Yes. Now what was Claire doing? Just a moment. Did she get up? No. She put her black bag and her case under her chair and waited — a bit like in the theatre, come to think of it. Yes, without getting up she shifted her chair round so as to face the bar.

Someone asked the detective what he thought about the crime. He said in his view the murderer was somebody from Viorne. And that's how it started.

* Tr.: The *préfecture de la Seine* — "Seine" for short — stands both for the *département* that includes Paris and for the French metropolitan police.

We were inventing a crime, we and he between us. The same crime as had just been committed. But we didn't recognize it. He made us talk, we said what he wanted us to say, we reconstructed the Viorne murder step by step. But we didn't notice.

I think we could start using the tape-recorder now.

— *We'll take up the conversation from where you've just left it. The detective had just said the murderer was somebody from Viorne.*

— Where was the tape-recorder?

— *In the brief-case on the floor.*

— When does the recording start?

— *From the moment it began its work — when Pierre came in.*

— Now you tell me I'm not all that surprised. He spoke very loud and fast.

— *Once he stood up he only had the length of one tape at his disposal — about an hour.*

We'll have the two tape-recorders running at the same time. The first will play back the conversation that evening. I'll stop it when you want to add anything. I'll leave the second machine running all the time so it'll record both the conversation and the comments.

Whenever Claire speaks please come in immediately afterwards to let the reader know it was her.

This is the point at which you left off.

.... said?

— He's a cop.

— So what do you really think yourself?

— I think it's somebody from Viorne. The reason's quite simple: if it had been someone else they wouldn't have come back three nights running to the same viaduct. If they'd made use of three different viaducts — and there are plenty of them about here — it would have been much more difficult to trace him. Practically impossible.

— So it's someone from Viorne.

— Ten to one, yes.

— So we're shut up in Viorne with the murderer?

— Probably, yes.

— What about the victim?

— She must have been murdered in Viorne. Again because of the nearness of the viaduct. If she'd been killed somewhere else, why should the murderer have come to Viorne to get rid of her? No, it's someone from Viorne, who did the murder at Viorne, and who had no way out, physically no way out for those three nights. You see where that leads us?

— Someone who hadn't got a car?

— Exactly.

— Nor a bike. Nothing. Someone who only had their two legs.

— Exactly. You might say we can already start to see the personality of the criminal through the crime.

— I haven't heard anybody say they'd have foreseen the catch about the intersections.

— A real killer, a professional, would have thought of it. So we already know what the murderer is not. He's not a professional killer, at any rate.

— But the fact that he solved his problem by throwing the pieces down on nine different trains — that implies a certain capacity for reflection, a certain intelligence, doesn't it?

— Yes, very likely — if it was deliberate.

— What sort of possibilities are left, then, apart from professional killers?

— There are those who might have thought of using different trains but didn't work it out any further. And those who didn't think or calculate at all, either about the time or about the number of trains, but just happened by chance on a different train every time.

— Most people, in fact?

— Yes. Chance was as likely to succeed in this case as calculation.

— What else do they know so far?

— That's Claire.

— They know it must be someone who's not very strong — physically, I mean. Someone strong wouldn't have needed to make so many journeys.

— That's true too. Perhaps it was just somebody old.

— Yes, or tired?

— Or ill?

— They're all possible. One might even go further still, if I'm not boring you. . .

— On the contrary. Go on.

— It's also very likely we're dealing with someone methodical. Conscientious.

— Did he say religious?

— That's Claire.

— Yes.

— Perhaps religious too. That may even be the most appropriate description, madame. Because of their not being able to find the head.

— I don't follow.

— If the murderer didn't throw away the

13

head like the rest, the first explanation you think of.is that it was to make identification impossible.

— Yes.

— Well, if you really think that about it you see it's more complicated than that.

— You mean if he was sure the viaduct trick would work he ought to have felt quite safe throwing the head away too? Is that it?

— Not exactly. What I mean is, given the panic he must have been in during the three nights he had to keep going backwards and forwards to the viaduct, and how fantastically tired he must have felt when you come to think of it, and how terrified of being caught before he'd finished, it's amazing that he should have been so calculating about the head. There's something inexplicable in his attitude. Either he thinks he's going to commit the perfect crime, in which case he mutilates the head and throws it away with the rest. Or he has some personal reason, some moral reason you might say, for giving the head special treatment. He might be a believer, for instance, or have been, once.

— I think you're stretching it a bit.

— Do you?

— But maybe all your theories will collapse when you find out the truth? You may be completely mistaken?

— Of course. But it would be surprising if we were wrong about absolutely everything. It doesn't often happen.

— So it all happened here?

— Yes. The mystery is in your keeping.

If you ask me, what we're dealing with here is a crime of impulse. Unpremeditated. Does that surprise you?

— Yes. The viaduct idea may not have been properly worked out but it must have taken some thinking of.

— Why? Why should it have been thought out in advance? Why shouldn't he have thought of it just as he was going over the viaduct with his bundle under his arm—perhaps after walking about for hours trying to decide what to do with it? It's you, the newspaper reader, who's invented the idea of the nine trains. When you come to think about it that idea can disappear and turn into pure chance.

— Why are you in favour of chance and against premeditation?

— Because there's a sort of naturalness about this murder that doesn't seem to go with calculation.

— A madman.

— What's the difference?

— Claire again. She sounds as if she's in another room.

— Between what and what?

— Between someone who's mad and someone normal — when it comes to murder. She means how can you tell whether it's a madman or not?

— The difference begins after the murder's been committed. You can say to yourself: a madman wouldn't have had such patience. A real madman wouldn't have trundled backwards and forwards regularly like an ant for three nights. On the other hand, a madman

15

might have held on to the head. Which is what happened.

— A madman might have talked perhaps? He might have talked already?

— No, you can't be sure.

— Has the murderer made any mistake, would you say?

— Yes. Criminals always make a mistake. But I can't tell you any more than that.

— Was the murderer mad or not?
— Her again. I'd forgotten she asked that.

— I don't know, madame.

Another thing we know is that the dead woman couldn't have been good-looking. She must have been very clumsily built, with great hefty shoulders. Stout. A sort of . . . animal.

— A worker?
— Yes.

— I seem to recognize someone, listening to that description. Silly really. . .

— Everyone does.

— What do you conclude from the fact that she wasn't good-looking?

— That it's a mistake to talk about a crime of passion.

— And no one's been reported missing?

— No. And probably no one will be. If it was going to happen it would have happened by now. The papers have been full of it for a week, and still not a word about anyone being missing. No, it must be someone without any family, and without any friends sufficiently interested to worry.

— Or someone living alone?

— Living alone where? If it had been in a flat the concierge would already have come rushing in to say so-and-so hadn't been seen for a week.

— What about someone living alone in a house then?

— Same thing. Some neighbour would have reported that so-and-so hadn't opened her shutters for a week, or hadn't been seen for a week and the dustbins had been left out all that time. And so on.

— What an imagination... Still, she must have lived somewhere, mustn't she?

— Of course. At least we can be certain of that...

Don't you see?

— You mean it was someone who was killed by the people she lived with?

— Precisely. Ten to one that's it. It's the only explanation for the silence about her disappearance.

You're in for some surprises in Viorne. I can tell that already. You can sense a murder from a distance, scent the sort of thing it is...

— And what sort of thing is it in this case? In your opinion, I mean.

— I know what you mean... In this case I think that the murderer killed the other person as if he were killing himself... It's true of lots of cases, you know.

— Because the murderer hated himself, or they hated each other?

17

— Not necessarily . . . perhaps because they were together in a situation that was too static and had been in existence too long. Not necessarily an unhappy situation in itself, but stuck, no way out, if you see what I mean.

— No one moves. We're all at the bar except Claire and Alfonso.

— Are you just guessing?

— I'm giving you my personal opinion. There's no such thing as a guess in our vocabulary. I arrived at my opinion by eliminating the two motives of gain and passion as unlikely. . .

— It's funny we can't think of anybody though. . .

— That's Pierre to Alfonso. Alfonso didn't answer.

— You know, these crimes that seem so strange from a distance come to look almost . . . natural, when you find out the truth. So natural you often can't see how the criminal could have avoided committing them.

— But butchery like this?

— As good a way as any of throwing people off the scent. Of course everyone's revolted, but once a person's dead, whether they're whole or in bits. . . What's more, we forget too easily what the murderer himself must have been through.

— Right, well, ladies and gentlemen, I must be off.

— But it's quite early, Alfonso. . .

— That's Claire. Alfonso gets up.

— You can understand anything if you try:

— What I say is, we shouldn't *try* to explain. If we start trying to explain where shall we

18

end up? We shouldn't even begin. We should just be satisfied with proof, that's all.

— No, Robert, I think it's always better to try to understand, to enter into the circumstances as far, as deeply as possible. Even if it means getting lost in them, you should always take them into account...

— To understand is such a happiness, Monsieur Lamy, such a real one, and it's so natural to want it that it's a sort of duty not to deprive anyone of it — anyone: the public, or even the lawyers, or even sometimes the criminals themselves.

— No, monsieur. You can't understand everything, it's impossible. So at a certain moment you have to call a halt. Stop trying. Otherwise, as I say, where shall we end up?

— Robert, you're wrong, I assure you.

— I agree with Monsieur Pierre. You're wrong, Robert.

— I agree with Monsieur Lamy.

— Robert, please...

— I wouldn't listen. What a fool you can be sometimes.

— Robert, you're usually so generous, so ready to understand, why do you suddenly talk like this? It's awful.

— Matter of life and death. The people of Seine-et-Oise are frightened. What about all the undesirables padding about the roads day and night?

— Robert...

— What?

— Nothing.

— I didn't understand what Alfonso was driving at. He sat down again and didn't say anything.

— People are never really safe from the

ideas that might come into their heads. No one can say: that's something I could never do. I remember a murder that was done once by an agricultural worker not far from here. Perfectly respectable chap from every point of view. One evening he was picking potatoes in a field and a woman went by. He'd known her for a long time. Perhaps he desired her, loved her even, without admitting it to himself? She wouldn't go with him into the forest, and he killed her. Ought *he* to be punished like any other murderer?

— Pierre turned and looked at Alfonso.
      — What happened?
      — They decided he'd had a sudden black-out. Let him off quite lightly. Ten years I think he got.
      — Perhaps when you get down to it the real cause of most crimes . . .
— Listen, Pierre's starting . . .
      . . . is just opportunity. Suppose you were living night and day near a . . . say an enormous bomb . . . and all you had to do to set it off was press a button. One fine day you just do it. You live with another person for years and years, and then one evening the idea occurs to you. At first you think that if you can have the idea you could actually do it—but of course you haven't any intention of doing it. Then you think to yourself that someone else in your shoes might do it, someone else who had good reason. And after that again you think to yourself that there's always good reason, always, and that someone else in your situation who wasn't so . . .

20

— weak?

— Every so often Pierre makes speeches. I thought he was trying to show off in front of the detective.

— ... yes, I suppose that's the word: someone else who wasn't so weak as you would do it. That's how it starts. And then the idea comes back to you more and more often, until one day it's there to stay. It gets bigger and bigger until it fills the whole house, you can't move without knocking into it. And there you are.

— What's he talking about?

— Claire, to Alfonso.

— Just some nonsense.

— And then one day you do it. And there you are. After that it's a different matter.

— I think Alfonso laughed then.

— I'm going on like this because I've got an idea. The same idea as this gentleman here. The same idea as you. And I want to say what it is.

— Please do.

— Not to you. I'd rather die.

— I came out from the bar and went over to Pierre. It was as if we were all detectives now. I wanted him to say what he thought, tell us what the cop was thinking.

— I'll tell you what it is. Pierre thinks the murder is like the one you were just telling us about — the one where the agricultural worker killed the woman — he thinks that's what's happened here in Viorne.

— Pierre didn't answer. I pressed him.

21

— Is that why you haven't been in for a week?

— No, that's not it.

— We all waited. Pierre didn't say any more. The detective started again.

— You think Monsieur Alfonso knows who did it, and won't say. That's what you think.

— We all turned and looked at Alfonso. Claire got up. Alfonso didn't move.

— What's the matter with you, Pierre? Have you gone crazy?

— I'm sorry, Robert.

— Where did you get that idea from?

— I spend too much time reading the papers, Robert. It looked to me as if Alfonso was hiding something, and all of a sudden I couldn't stand it.

— Is that why you stopped coming in?

— No, that's not it.

— Why then?

— None of your business.

— Alfonso got up and came over to Pierre. I'd never seen him angry.

— And supposing I had got an idea about the murder, Pierre? Do you want me to tell him what it is? What's the matter with you?

Answer me, Pierre.

— I suddenly wanted to know. I couldn't resist.

— May I offer everyone another drink? The same again all round, please, Monsieur Robert.

— It's obvious you don't often foot the bill,

monsieur. But we're not the people to refuse a drink.

— Come on now, let's forget it.
— Pierre was stricken by what he'd done. Alfonso had stopped being angry and had come and put his hand on Pierre's shoulder. Claire just stood there and watched them.
— Everyone knows you can't sleep at night and so you go walking about in the forest. You see, you know everyone, and you live in the forest, and somehow I can't get it out of my head that that was where it happened. So I thought you must at least have some idea. And then with the detective leading me on. . .
— That'll do, Pierre.
— All right.

— Monsieur Alfonso hasn't told us whether Monsieur Pierre was right.
— We all looked at Alfonso again.
— *Did Claire still not move?*
— I believe she did, but towards the detective already.

— It was all my imagination. Leave him alone.
— I don't intend to question Monsieur Alfonso. Don't worry. I was just making a remark.

— You go home, Alfonso.
— No.
— And then Pierre started again.

— You might say something.
— They'll find out what they want without my help. Won't you, monsieur?

23

— That can only mean you know as well as I do that the murder was committed in Viorne?

On the night of the 7th to the 8th of April?

And in the forest, near your place, fifty yards from the viaduct, at the top of the railway bank?

— Alfonso didn't answer. He laughed. There was a long silence. Then he answered.
        — That's right. In the forest, about fifty yards from the viaduct. I heard the sound of the blows.
— Claire moved now. She went right over to the detective. We'd all forgotten about her.
        — It wasn't in the forest.

        — That's enough of all this. Either some-one's got something to say or they keep their mouth shut. No point in starting something and then clamming up. Let's change the subject, or I'll close for the night.

        — What are you talking about, Claire? Claire?

        — It wasn't in the forest.

        — Take no notice of her, monsieur, she's going right round the bend, this time I'm sure of it. Of course you can't be expected to know but as her husband I can assure you. . .
        — What was it you wanted to tell me, madame?
— Pierre got hold of Claire and dragged her away from

the detective. But she came back again. The detective stood there calm and smiling.

— You wanted to say something, madame?

— Yes.

— Then the girl stepped in. It was her turn now.

— It's very difficult, isn't it, madame?

You wanted to say something about your cousin, Marie-Thérèse Bousquet, didn't you, madame?

— Then we all knew. We were stunned.

— But how . . . ?

How did you know about her?

— We know about everyone.

— But Marie-Thérèse Bousquet has gone away, monsieur, what's the matter with you?

— Pierre, I'm going to shut!

— We've got plenty of time, haven't we, madame?

— I tell you I'm closing, Pierre!

— No, you're not closing. Come over here with me, madame.

— Pierre, Pierre, I'm closing!

— Alfonso didn't say anything. He just looked at Claire.

— But what's the matter with you? Marie-Thérèse has gone to Cahors. Claire will tell you. Claire!

— Can you tell us *how* Marie-Thérèse went, madame?

— She won't answer you, monsieur, she

never answers questions, just let her speak by herself. Claire!

You see, she won't answer you any more. Anyway how can it possibly interest you? I suppose Marie-Thérèse just packed her case and took the coach to the Gare d'Austerlitz. The idea just came into her head one fine morning, that's all...
— Did you see her go?
— It's just that no one knew she'd gone, you see, Pierre, so we were a bit taken by surprise. But of course you saw her go, didn't you...? I was just thinking, well, well, it's a long time since I saw Marie-Thérèse...
— Pierre... tell us.
— She'll be back from Cahors, you know, monsieur. Won't she, Claire? You see, she doesn't answer... you have to get to know her... oh yes... But she told me all about it... they said goodbye to each other at the door. Claire stayed there till the bus left. Tell him, Claire!

— Alfonso! Alfonso!

Alfonso!
— Alfonso made to go. Claire called him back.

— Alfonso!
— Don't be frightened, madame. I'm here to take care of you. Tell us what you have to say.

— Claire! Claire!
— Pierre's trying to prevent her from saying anything.
— Claire!

— And then everyone else was silent, and Claire spoke.
— It wasn't in the forest that Marie-Thérèse was killed. It was in a cellar, at four o'clock in the morning.

— We knew it was Marie-Thérèse Bousquet, but we didn't know which one of you three had killed her.

There were words written on the pieces of the body, in coal. "Cahors", and "Alfonso". The papers weren't allowed to mention it.

Come with us, madame.

— *Pierre Lannes didn't ever speak to you about his wife?*
— No, never. I don't think he did to anyone. But Alfonso and I knew.
—*What?*
— That some day or another she'd go out of her mind completely and Pierre would finally have to leave her.
It was really as if she'd been thrown into the detective's arms.
— *Did she say anything after that?*
— No. She just let them take her away.
She was fascinated by the man. She stared at him all the time she was speaking to him — it was if he was dictating the words to her one by one.
— *You sound rather as if you didn't altogether believe in Claire's confession?*
You don't have to answer my questions if you prefer not to.
— In that case I won't answer that one.
— *If you'd thought she was guilty, before, would you, Robert Lamy, have shielded her from the police?*

27

— I prefer not to answer.

— *Do you think if Alfonso had thought she was guilty he would have shielded her from the police?*

— Yes.

— *And yet Alfonso did hardly anything that evening to protect her?*

— As you heard, he said at one point that he was going, and she said it was quite early, and he stayed. And another time — at the end — she called out "Alfonso" as if she were shouting for help. That second time he was going towards the door again.

But it's true he might have done more. He could have taken her with him, she would have gone. But he didn't.

If he didn't it's because he didn't know anything, didn't know she was in danger of being arrested. That strikes me as perfectly natural.

— *Or perhaps he was afraid that if he pressed her to go she'd show everyone how crazy she was. That she'd ask him why he wanted to go, and say too much.*

— I didn't think of that.

Perhaps it was there in the Balto, while the detective was talking, that he realized. Before the rest of us, but too late to do anything. If you ask me we shall never know what he knew and what he didn't know.

— *Why do you think he confirmed the lie the detective told about where the crime took place?*

— To take the rise out of him. He was laughing when he said he'd heard the sound of the blows on the banks of the viaduct. He would have confirmed anything.

— *But wasn't that a dangerous thing for him to do?*

— No. Pierre and I can both testify that he was only making fun of the detective. Didn't he tell them that himself when he was interrogated?

— *I believe so.*

— Well then.

— *Did you think the detective was wrong in what he said?*

— No, I thought it was the truth. I think Alfonso was the only one who knew the detective was just inventing the place where the crime was supposed to have been committed. In the first place he does live in the forest. Then as he was only watching the conversation as a sort of spectator he must have seen the lie being slipped in. Make no mistake, if Alfonso had really known where the murder was committed he would have kept quiet.

— *I'm not so sure about that. Nor are you, I think.*

— But how could he have known that the word "forest" would start her off?

— *What other conclusions do you come to after hearing the tape?*

— It sounded as if everyone started to be afraid for her very early on, as soon as she came into the café and saw the detective. But it wasn't really like that. People were afraid, but not in the way you might think now. They were just afraid the detective might notice she was a bit touched. No more than that.

— *And that her attitude might make him suspect her?*

— That it might make him suspect one of us. How should we ever have thought of her?

I don't mind telling you I personally am glad Alfonso has left the country. He would have had a job keeping himself out of trouble.

I'm going to clear out of Viorne too. I can't stand the sight of it.

— *Why did you tell me you were all afraid the detective might think Claire was mad?*

— In case he'd said we all seemed a bit odd that evening — like people all afraid of the same thing. Like people with a secret.

— *You speak as if you all had to make common cause against the police.*

— That's natural enough.

— *The detective only said one thing: that Alfonso hardly said anything during the first part of the evening — he just looked at Claire.*

— He hardly ever did say anything, though of course the police couldn't be expected to know that. So you see we were quite right to be careful.

— *You yourself were most afraid on Alfonso's account?*

— I suppose so, but without quite realizing.

— *What impression did Pierre Lannes make on you?*

— I told you what I thought at the time — I thought he looked worried. Now, I'd go further and say he looked afraid. But there again I can easily go wrong. The most obvious explanation would be that he was afraid all the evening that Claire would say something about Marie-Thérèse having gone to Cahors. Now I know — I can't help it, there's no blinking the fact — that she'd spoken to him about it the morning after the murder, I tend to think that was what he was afraid of. But I know that's not right, I'm sure of it.

What he must really have been afraid of was what was going to happen now that the cousin had gone and left him alone with Claire. What was going to become of them. That was all.

I'm just thinking aloud when I say all this.

— *You didn't ever visit the Lannes?*

— No, never. People don't entertain much in a village. That's not to say they don't know a good deal about each other — nearly all there is to know, in fact.

— *You don't find it strange that Pierre Lannes should say he wouldn't have thought of the trap about the intersections?*

— No. Everybody said the same.

— Has he changed recently, in your opinion? Morally, I mean.

— For the past few years he hasn't been quite the same as he used to be.

You probably know he stood for the municipal elections in Viorne? Yes. Five years ago. He didn't get in. It was a great disappointment to him.

I don't think he'll say anything to you about it. He had a passion for politics. He'd stayed out of them for a long time, then one day he put up as candidate. He had a very good name in Viorne and he thought there wouldn't be any difficulty. But he was wrong.

— Was it partly to do with his wife that he wasn't elected?

— Is that what you've been told?

— No. What do you think?

— That's what some people said. But others thought it was because he was already a bit old for it. Too fond of the ladies, too, some people said.

— What do you know about her?

— Her? Everyone could see her sitting there on her bench in the garden. Recently she didn't even see you half the time when you went by. And everyone knew how lazy she was, and that Marie-Thérèse Bousquet did all the work there.

It must happen more often than people think, that a village has a harmless lunatic or so and doesn't take any notice. Until the disaster happens.

— You don't know anything about her life before she came to Viorne?

— No. I know what happened in Viorne. I know, for instance, as a lot of people do, that he was often unfaithful to her and she didn't care in the least. But about when they were in Cahors, when they were young, I don't know anything at all.

— What do you know that other people don't?

— That he wasn't happy.

— *Because of her?*

— No — not only that — she didn't occupy such an important place in his life. Because he was getting old and wouldn't be able to have the affaires he used to. He couldn't get over that, I knew, though of course he didn't say anything.

— *Was he perhaps ashamed of his wife?*

— I don't think ashamed is the word. She wasn't the sort of person you'd be ashamed of. He must have been afraid of what she might say, and that people might think she was touched, but only in front of strangers. Not with us. Whenever she started droning on we just let her talk. Sometimes Alfonso listened to her. Pierre and I would just go on talking to each other.

Sometimes the four of us would stay on together after the café was shut. I liked talking to him. He's no fool and he always knows what's going on. He's a good sort; he was always as calm and sensible as she was crazy.

— *What did she use to talk about, when she did talk?*

— Oh everything. What she'd seen in the street or on television. She had a way of telling things that made Alfonso laugh, and she knew this and often used to tell him about the films she'd seen on television. I must admit I hadn't got the patience to listen to her. It bored me. Pierre too. But not Alfonso. It just depended on the person, I suppose.

— *What ... sort of thing did she use to say?*

— Ten different things at once. Floods of words. And then suddenly silence.

— *Without head or tail to it?*

— No, because Alfonso, for example, could follow. But you'd need to pay close attention. Sometimes Alfonso used to tell me: "You ought to listen to what she says." I did try, but I never once stuck it out till she'd finished.

— *What she said did have a beginning and an end then?*

— Yes, I expect so, but you couldn't make them out. Before you knew where you were she was off in all directions, everything would connect with everything else in ways that would never have occurred to you.

— *But she never talked about any particular person in Viorne?*

— Very rarely. It was always either the paper or the television or her own ideas. Or rather that was what she'd start from.

— *Was it the talk of a madwoman?*

— I don't know. I can't bring myself to use the word even now.

— *You just referred to harmless lunatics that people in a village don't take any notice of.*

— That was just an expression.

— *And you said you knew that one day she'd go out of her mind completely.*

— Yes. But just the same, if you ask me to say outright once and for all whether it was madness or not, I can't tell you. In another house, with different people, with another man, things might have turned out differently. Who knows?

— *She was considered intelligent in spite of this sort of craziness she had?*

— Yes, by Alfonso anyway. He used to say that if she'd managed to be reasonable she'd have been very clever. Nobody else bothered to ask themselves the question. If you ask me, Pierre was the more intelligent of the two.

— *Did you see Alfonso again before he went back to Italy?*

— Yes. He came to see me the day before he went. Three days ago, that is. We talked about this and that and in the course of conversation he told me he was leaving France the next morning.

— *And you didn't ask him any questions about what had happened?*

33

— I wouldn't have dreamed of such a thing. Besides, I knew that even if he was implicated he was innocent.

— *What did you talk about?*

— What he was going to do when he got back to Modena. And a bit about her — about Claire. He told me that ten years ago he was fond of her and if it hadn't been for Pierre he'd have taken her to live with him in his cottage. That was the first time he ever mentioned it to me. I never knew anything about it.

— *Did he regret not having done it?*

— He didn't talk about regrets.

— *Didn't you ask him why he was going away?*

— There was no point. I knew. He was going away because he was afraid of what Claire might say to the police, of what she might make up so as to get him sent to prison too. Everything was against him: agricultural labourer, living alone, foreigner into the bargain. He thought the best thing to do was just go.

— *Did he know she'd try to involve him?*

— Yes. Oh, he knew she wouldn't do it out of malice. It would be out of . . . madness — I only use that word for want of another. You see, since she was going to prison, she'd probably want him to go too. She was very attached to him.

— *And he to her?*

— Yes.

Perhaps she thought they might both be put in the same prison? Who knows? Perhaps she'll say what she thought.

— *How did Alfonso know this — among other things?*

— I don't know. But he knew.

— *Without ever having talked to her about it?*

— I don't see when they could have spoken alone.

— *You knew she used to go out at night sometimes?*

— I know because he told the police she did. I read it in the paper. That's all I know about it.

— *Well, as he was in the habit of prowling about at*

34

night too — apparently he didn't sleep much — they must have met and talked?

— Possibly. But I only speak of what I know. And I've never seen them together except in the Balto when Pierre was there — never alone and never anywhere else.

In my opinion there was never anything between them even before.

— Would he have told you about it if there was?

— No, he wouldn't. But just the same I don't believe there was anything.

— She said they met each other during the third night after the murder. He says they didn't. What are we to think?

— Well, you know, if he lied to the police it was really just to try to save her. So it doesn't count. It's quite understandable. He wanted to protect her.

— So the last evening Alfonso came into the café you didn't talk about the murder?

— No. We talked about her, as I said, but only in the past.

— You don't think it strange that you didn't say a single word about the murder?

— No.

— Why shouldn't Claire have told Alfonso that she'd killed Marie-Thérèse Bousquet?

Why should she have avoided telling him just that? When she knew she could depend on him?

—When could she have told him?

— During that night, in Viorne?

— But he says he didn't see her. Of the two I prefer to believe him.

May I ask you one or two questions?

— Yes.

— What does what I've said tell you about the murder?

— It doesn't tell me anything about the murder, except that you have the same doubts as I have about Claire's

35

guilt. But what you've said does tell me something very important about Claire. It tells me she was much less isolated in Viorne than one might have thought: she was protected by Alfonso, and to a certain extent by you.

— But still she was alone, as a mad person always is alone, no matter where.

— *Yes, but hers wasn't the sort of madness that cut her off from the world completely and made everyone indifferent to her.*

— I'm really answering all these questions for Alfonso's sake, you know. Just for her I wouldn't have done it. I hadn't any personal connection with her. She used to come to the café often enough, like a lot of other people, and when you keep seeing people you think you know them; but there's knowing and knowing. Alfonso, Pierre — yes, I knew them. But not her. I might as well tell you that as a woman I never found her attractive.

— *Did you talk to Alfonso about her as if she were mad?*

— No, just as a woman in the first place — a woman who was a bit crazy in some ways, but not as someone who was mad first and foremost. We never used the word "mad" when we were talking about her. It would have been tantamount to passing sentence on her. We'd have used the word of other people, who weren't mad at all, before we'd have used it of her.

My second question is this: why are you interested in whether or not Alfonso knew what Claire had done?

— *I'm trying to find out what sort of a woman Claire Lannes really is, and why she says she committed this murder. She can't give any reason for having done it. So I'm looking for a reason for her. And I think that if anyone knows anything about it it's Alfonso.*

Assuming, of course, that she's guilty, I work it out like this: either Alfonso knows everything, and if he let her be arrested it was because he saw no hope of her emerging from her madness and thought it better she should be shut up; or he didn't really know what had happened, he only suspected, and if he let her be arrested it was because he too wanted to put an end to something.

— What?

— Say Claire's situation in general.

— I believe I see what you mean.

— Perhaps he let her be arrested for the same reason as she committed the murder. Then they'd both have done the same thing, she by committing the crime and he by letting her be arrested.

— Wasn't that love, then?

— What is the right name for such an enormous sympathy? It could have taken the form of love, but it might just as well have taken lots of others.

— Although they never spoke to each other?

— Yes, apparently.

What was there between Marie-Thérèse Bousquet and Alfonso?

— Nothing except that they used to sleep together now and again. He wasn't the sort to be put off by the fact that she was deaf and dumb.

— Nor by the fact that Claire was mad?

— Nor that either.

Would you have questioned Alfonso if he'd stayed in Viorne?

— No. He wouldn't have said anything. He didn't tell the police anything about her except her walking about at night.

— No, you're right — he wouldn't have said anything. You're convinced he knew something, aren't you?

— Yes. But I don't know what.

What do you think?

— He must have known something in general, but not what actually happened. But telling about it, even if he'd wanted to — that's another matter.

37

Will you see Pierre and Claire?
— *Yes.*

— Have you any idea about the motives for the crime?
—*There's something dimly visible, but it's impossible to say what.*
— That sounds as if you thought Claire was guilty.
— *No, I'm just talking about what she says. Whether she just says she committed the murder or whether she really did it, her motives would be the same — if only she could give them.*

Have you noticed that we haven't said anything about one thing that happened that evening?
— Yes.
— *You said a little while ago that Pierre must have been afraid all evening that Claire would say something about Marie-Thérèse having gone away.*
— Yes, I remember.
— *Is "afraid" the right word?*
— I don't know.

— *If anyone threw Claire into the arms of the police, who was it? Pierre or Alfonso?*
— If I didn't know him I'd have said it was Pierre.
— *And as you do know him?*
— As I do know him I'd say he was ready to throw the whole of Viorne into the arms of the police that evening.
— *Who do you think Pierre Lannes would have killed with that enormous bomb that he spoke of?*
— Himself.
— *If I had a different opinion from yours about Pierre Lannes' attitude that evening, would you want to know about it?*
— No.

38

II

— *I've asked you to come here to answer some questions about your wife Claire Lannes.*
— Why?
— *To help with a book about the murder recently committed in Viorne.*
— How?
— *We're using a tape-recorder. It's on now.*
I've already talked to Robert Lamy.
You can answer my questions or not just as you like.

— All right.
—*Would you please introduce yourself?*

— My name's Pierre Lannes. I was born in Cahors. I'm fifty-seven. I'm a civil servant in the Ministry of Finance.
— *You've lived in Viorne since 1944 — twenty-two years.*
— Yes. Apart from two years in Paris after we were married we've always lived here.
— *You married Claire Bousquet in Cahors in 1942.*
— Yes.

— *As you probably know, she told the police she committed the murder alone and you didn't know anything about it.*
— That's the truth.
— *You found out at the same time as the police did?*
— Yes. I found out everything when she confessed in the café Balto on the evening of April 13.

41

— *Before that evening, during the five days after the murder, you hadn't the slightest suspicion of what had happened?*

— No. Not the slightest.

— *I should like you to tell me how she explained the absence of her cousin, Marie-Thérèse Bousquet.*

— She said: "Marie-Thérèse went back to Cahors first thing this morning." That was about seven o'clock, when I got up.

— *Did you believe her?*

— I didn't believe she was telling the whole truth, but I thought she was telling part of it. I didn't think she was lying.

— *Did you always believe what she told you?*

— Yes. Everyone who knew her believed her.

I thought that although she might have lied to me once about some things in her past, she didn't lie to me at all any more.

— *What do you mean, her past?*

— Before we met. But that was a long time ago, nothing to do with the murder.

— *You weren't surprised to hear your cousin had gone away?*

— Yes, I was very surprised. But to tell you the truth the first thing I thought of was the house — what a mess everything would get into while she was away. Terrible. I asked Claire a bit more about it, and she told me a perfectly convincing story. She said Marie-Thérèse had gone because she wanted to see her father again before he died, and she'd be back in a few days.

— *And after a few days, did you remind her?*

— Yes. And she said: "We're just as well without her. I've written and told her not to come back." I didn't say anything.

— *You still believed her?*

— I still thought she was hiding something but I still didn't think she was actually lying.

I didn't try to find out the whole truth. The mere fact that Marie-Thérèse wouldn't be coming back was depressing enough.

— *But various suppositions must have crossed your mind?*

— Yes. The only one that seemed likely was that Marie-Thérèse had gone off because she'd suddenly had enough of us — us, and Viorne, and the house — and didn't like to say so. It seemed to me the excuse about her father was just a tactful way of getting out of it.

— *You knew Marie-Thérèse well. What other explanations occurred to you?*

— I thought she might have gone off with a man, a Portuguese — it was all one to the Portuguese her being deaf and dumb, they can't speak the language anyway.

— *Might she have gone away with Alfonso?*

— No. No, even before, there was no question of feeling between her and Alfonso. It was just a matter of convenience, if you see what I mean.

One thing that never even crossed my mind was that Claire and Marie-Thérèse might have quarrelled.

— *What did you decide to do?*

— I was going to have Claire put into a nursing-home and then go to Cahors after Marie-Thérèse. Then I'd have been able to tell her I was on my own now and there wouldn't be so much work.

— *In other words Marie-Thérèse's going was a godsend for you — just the opportunity you needed to be able to leave Claire.*

— Yes. A blessing in disguise, but still a blessing. A blessing I'd never dared to hope for, even.

— *And supposing Marie-Thérèse hadn't wanted to come*

43

back even though Claire wasn't there any more? Did you think of that?

— Yes. I'd have got someone else. I'd have had to. I can't keep house for myself.

— *But you'd still have got rid of Claire in the same way as if Marie-Thérèse had come back?*

— Yes, with all the more reason really, because someone new wouldn't have put up with Claire in the house.

— *And it was because of all this you didn't try to find out any more about Marie-Thérèse's departure?*

— Perhaps. But another reason is that I hardly saw Claire during those five days. It was fine, she stayed in the garden. I did the shopping when I came home from work.

— *Didn't she eat anything?*

— No, she wouldn't. I think she must have had something during the night. She must have eaten something some time, and one morning there wasn't so much bread left as there should have been.

— *Did she seem very low during those five days?*

— When I went out she was in the garden. When I came back she was still out there. I hardly saw her. But I don't think she seemed low. I'm talking about the five days after the murder. I'm a bit confused about the dates. During the time it was all going on, if I remember rightly, I found her asleep one day on the bench in the garden. She looked exhausted. The next day she went to Paris. I found her all dressed up at about two in the afternoon and she said she was going to Paris. She got back late, about ten that night. That must be a week ago now, it was five days before the evening in the Balto, the Saturday.

— *In other words it was the day before the last night she spent in the cellar?*

— If we've worked it out properly, yes.

— *She didn't go to Paris very often?*

— Not for the last few years.

Apart from that trip to Paris, whether it was during or after the crime, she must have spent all her time in the garden.

— *I understand she always spent a good deal of time in the garden. So what was the difference?*

— None, really . . . except that nothing was done at any special time in the house after Marie-Thérèse had gone, so she could stay out there as long as she liked, until it was dark.

— *Didn't you call her in?*

— I didn't feel like it any more.

To tell you the truth I'd been a bit scared of her for some time, ever since she chucked the transistor down the well. It seemed to me that must be the beginning of the end.

— *It wasn't suspicion as well as fear?*

— I wasn't suspicious about anything that had already happened. How could anyone imagine such a thing?

— *Have you seen her since she was arrested?*

— Yes, the next day — I went to the prison and they let me see her.

— *What impression does she make on you now?*

— I don't understand anything any more, even about myself.

— *What was it you were afraid of?*

— With Marie-Thérèse not there I was afraid of everything.

— *She used to keep an eye on her then?*

— Oh yes. She had to. In the nicest possible way, of course, don't worry. I was afraid she'd create a scandal, do herself in. . . You know, after a thing like this happens you think you can remember thinking things that may never have entered your head.

— *You didn't go down to the cellar during those days?*

— I do go down during the winter to fetch wood. But the weather was so warm then we didn't light the fire. Besides, without my saying anything, one day when I was just walking through the garden on my way out she said: "Don't waste your time going down to the cellar — Marie-Thérèse has taken the key away with her."

— *Were you afraid she'd kill herself, or do you really mean you hoped she would?*

— I can't remember.

— *Can you remember that evening in the Balto? You said some very . . . curious things.*

— Yes. I remember very well.

I still can't understand what got into me.

— *We'll come back to that if you don't mind.*

I'd like to know what you think: did she do it on her own, or did someone help her?

— On her own, I'm sure. How could it have been otherwise?

— *Apparently she says she met Alfonso one night about two o'clock, when she was on her way to the viaduct with her shopping-bag.*

— In that case I don't know, then.

Did they question Alfonso before he went?

— *Yes. He denied having seen her since the murder. But he said that for years he often used to come across her in the village at night.*

— Really? That's impossible.

— *Unless Alfonso is lying?*

— No, if he says it it's true.

— *What did she use to say about Alfonso?*

— She never talked about him any more than about anyone else. But when he used to come to chop wood she was always pleased. She used to say: "Thank God for Alfonso." That's all.

— *As you know, I'm not interested so much in the facts as in what underlies them. What's important to me is what you think about her.*

— I understand.

— *Why do you think she said she'd met Alfonso?*

— She was very fond of him, so normally you'd expect her not to mention it in case it got him into trouble. I don't understand it.

— *Do you understand why she was fond of Alfonso?*

— He was a decent chap who lived in a shack up in the wood. He didn't talk much either. He's Italian, lives on his own. But in Viorne they said he was a bit . . . well, simple . . . Claire must have imagined things about him, otherwise no, I don't see why she should have been so attached to him.

— *Weren't they a bit alike?*

— Perhaps, when you get right down to it. But she was sharper than he was.

I don't think they said the same about her in Viorne as they said about him. But I may be wrong.

What *do* they say about her? Have you asked?

— *Now they say what people always say: one day sooner or later . . . she was bound actually to do something . . . etc. I don't know what they said before. But I haven't heard anyone say you weren't happy with her.*

— I've always hidden the truth.

— *What truth?*

— Oh, about the life I led with her. She'd shown nothing but complete indifference for years.

For years she hadn't even looked at us. At meals she never even raised her eyes. When she spoke to us it was as if she was trying to lift some weight, as if she'd been frightened. As if she knew us less and less as time went by. Sometimes I used to think it was having Marie-Thérèse

47

there that got her into the habit of not talking, and I've even been sorry I brought her. But what else could I do? She'd never do anything. As soon as meals were over she'd go back into the garden, or else to her room, depending on the weather. For years and years.

— *What did she do in the garden or in her room?*

— If you ask me she just slept.

— *Didn't you ever go to see her or talk to her?*

— No, it would never even have occurred to me. You'd have to have lived with her to understand. When people have been married for a long time they don't have much to say to each other, but we had even less than most. Every so often of course I had to talk to her — I always made a point of telling her when anything out of the way had to be bought, or anything needed doing to the house. She always agreed to everything. Especially repairs. She loved having a workman in the house. She'd follow him about everywhere and watch him working. Sometimes it was a bit embarrassing for him, at least the first day, but after that he wouldn't take any notice. What it amounted to was that you had a sort of madwoman in the house, but harmless. Perhaps that's why we didn't take as much care as we ought to have done. Yes, I think that must be it. No need to look for any other explanation.

You know, it's got to the point where I wonder if she didn't make it all up, if it really was her who killed that poor girl. . .

— *It was her. The finger-prints correspond. There's no getting away from it.*

— I know.

But where could a woman have got the strength? If it weren't for the proofs, would you be able to believe it yourself?

— *Nobody would. Perhaps she wouldn't herself.*

She says that once — she didn't say when — she asked you if you had ever dreamed you were committing a murder. Do you remember?

— The magistrate's already asked me that. It was two or three years ago, I think. One morning. I have a vague recollection that she said something about dreaming of a murder. I must have said it had happened to me the same as to everyone else. She must have asked me why. I don't remember what I told her.

— You weren't particularly struck by the incident?

— No.

— And you were telling the truth when you said it had happened to you too?

— Yes. Once especially. It was a nightmare.

— When?

— I don't really remember. Not long before she asked me, I think.

— Who was it in the nightmare?

— It was a bit like what I was telling them about in the Balto the evening she confessed: I pressed a button, there was an explosion, and ...

— Remember you don't have to answer if you don't want to.

— I know.

But I must this time. It was Marie-Thérèse Bousquet.

But all the time, in the nightmare, I was crying because I saw I'd made a mistake and was killing the wrong person. I didn't really know who I was supposed to be killing, but I knew it wasn't Marie-Thérèse. I don't think it was my wife either.

— Haven't you tried to remember who it was?

— Yes, but I couldn't.

All that's got nothing to do with what's happened. Why are you asking me all these questions about it?

*— Let me remind you you don't have to answer if you
don't want to.*

*I'm trying to find out why your wife killed Marie-
Thérèse Bousquet. I observe that you both killed the same
person, you in dream, she in reality: the best-disposed
person in the world towards both of you.*

— But I knew I was making a mistake.

*— I don't think the mistake was part of your dream. I
think you must have made the correction immediately
afterwards.*

— But how?

*— In a second dream. It was in the second dream that
you cried.*

— That's possible. I can't answer for what I dream.

*— Of course not. In any case I don't think it was the
same crime you both committed through Marie-Thérèse,
you in dream and she in reality. Your real victims must
have been different.*

*Who was the victim in the story you told on the evening
of the confession?*

— There wasn't anybody. I just told them the outline of
the dream.

— Did you tell your wife the details of your dream?

— I should think not.

— Why?

— I never told her things like that. If I spoke to her
about it at all it was just to satisfy her, because she'd asked
me. I'd never have said anything about it off my own bat.

We hardly spoke to each other any more, especially to-
wards the end. I didn't even tell her when I was going out.
And then it took ages to explain the simplest thing to her.
You'd be a couple of hours trying to make her understand.

— For example?

— Anything. Everything. And then. . .

— Yes?

— She hadn't any discretion, she didn't realise there are some things you don't repeat. If I'd told her my dream about Marie-Thérèse she'd have been quite capable of talking about it at the table right in front of the poor thing.

— *But she couldn't hear?*

— She could lip-read. You knew that, didn't you?

— *Yes, I ought to have remembered.*

— She didn't miss anything you said. She was interested in everything. You only had to explain anything once to her, and she had a marvellous memory. Whereas my wife would just forget everything from one day to the next, and you'd have to start explaining all over again.

I had a very lonely life with her. Now it's all over I can say it.

— *But did she forget everything completely like that?*

— No, of course not, I was over-simplifying. She had her own kind of memory. Cahors, for instance — she remembered Cahors as if she'd only left it yesterday. Yes, she remembered that all right.

— *Were you often unfaithful to her?*

— Any man would have been unfaithful to her. I would have gone mad if I hadn't. Anyhow she must have known about it and she didn't care.

— *What about her?*

— I don't think she was ever unfaithful to me. Not out of fidelity but because everything was all the same to her. Even at the beginning, when we . . . well, you know what I mean . . . even then I had the . . . feeling that someone else would have served the purpose as well as me as far as she was concerned.

— *So she might easily have gone from one man to another?*

— Yes. But she might just as easily have stayed with the same one. I happened to be there.

— *Can you give me an example of the sort of thing she couldn't understand?*

— She didn't understand anything to do with the imagination. A story, or a play on the radio, for example — you could never make her see that it hadn't actually happened. She was a child in some ways.

She understood television. After her own fashion, of course. But at least she didn't ask questions about it.

— *Did she read the papers?*

— She used to say she did, but I'm not sure. She'd read the headlines and then leave it. I know her, and I tell you she didn't read the papers.

— *She just pretended to?*

— No, she didn't. She never pretended about anything. Not she. She thought she read the papers, but that's a different matter. Once, it must be a good ten years ago, she suddenly had a craze for reading. But just trash, children's comics. But after that she stopped.

I must admit it was because of me she stopped reading. It used to get on my nerves, quite apart from being a bit frightening. She was a cleaner at the school and she used to pinch the comics out of the children's desks. I said she wasn't to bring them home, and when she did I tore them up. So she gave it up.

So it was because of me she stopped reading the comics. I must have upset her but it was for her own good.

Afterwards she could have read as many of them as she liked as far as I was concerned, only she didn't want to any more by then. Ah well. How sad it all is. Poor woman.

— *Who?*

— Claire. My wife.

One day I made her read a book.

It was about the same time as the comics. I made her read aloud, a bit every evening. It was a travel book, I can remember it quite plainly. It was amusing as well as educational. But it was no good. I gave up in the middle.

I really believe the first half of that book was the only serious reading she ever did in her whole life.

— *Didn't it interest her?*

— Well, the thing was, she didn't see the point of learning, didn't know how to, she could only fix her mind on one thing at a time. While you were studying one country she'd completely forget the one you'd done the night before.

It used to upset me at first. Then I just let it go. It's no use keeping on at someone who doesn't want to alter.

— *What sort of education did you have?*

— I took the first part of the *baccalauréat*. I passed an exam and I'm an inspector in the registry. I had to leave school early because my father died and I had to go out to work. But I've always tried to keep up with things. I like reading.

— *Would you say she hadn't any intelligence?*

— No. I wouldn't say that. Some of her judgements were very shrewd. All of a sudden she'd come out with some remark on someone that would quite astonish you. And sometimes — when she was in one of her moods — she could be very funny. She and Marie-Thérèse used to lark about sometimes pretending they were mad. That was at the beginning, when Marie-Thérèse had just come. How long ago it seems.

And sometimes she used to talk very strangely, rather as if she were reciting something out of one of those modern books, whereas of course. . .

I can remember one or two things she said, about the flowers in the garden. She used to say: "The English mint is thin, and dark; it smells of fish, and comes from the Sandy Islands."

— *What would you have done if you'd stayed on at school?*
— I'd have liked to go into industry.

— *You said she hadn't got any imagination — or have I got it wrong?*
— You've got it wrong. I meant she couldn't understand other people's imagination. She herself had a very powerful imagination, there's no doubt about that. It must have occupied the most important place in her life.
— *And didn't you know anything about what went on in her imagination?*
— Practically nothing. . . But what I can tell you is that the stories she invented could really have happened. They always started off from something true — she didn't invent everything. It was afterwards they'd go off in all directions. For instance, sometimes she'd go on at me for reproaching her about things I never used to mention, especially towards the end. But they were things I could quite well have reproached her for if I'd wanted to. It was as if she'd seen into my mind.

And sometimes she'd tell us about conversations she thought she'd had with people in the street. You'd never have guessed she was inventing it until suddenly she made someone say something completely crazy.
— *You don't think she was unhappy about getting old?*
— No, not at all. That was one of the best things about her. Quite a comfort sometimes.
— *How did you know?*
— I knew.

— *What's your opinion about her?*
— You mean about her intelligence?
— *Yes, if you like.*

— You couldn't get anything into her. It was impossible for her to learn anything.

She didn't need to learn anything, anything at all. She could only understand what she could interpret in terms of herself — don't ask me how. It was as if she was closed to everything and open to everything at one and the same time. You couldn't get anything into her to stay, she retained nothing. Like a place without any doors, where the wind blows through and sweeps everything away. When I realised that she couldn't help it I gave up trying to teach her.

I still can't make out how she ever learned to read and write.

— *Would it be true to say she had no curiosity?*

— No, that wouldn't be true either. The thing was, her curiosity was of a peculiar kind. She was intrigued by people en bloc, not by the details of what they might say or do. I believe Marie-Thérèse interested her like that for quite a time. Especially at the beginning. She used to wonder how she managed to live. She wondered that about Alfonso too.

— *Did she become Alfonso or Marie-Thérèse?*

— Almost. She cut wood for two days so as to be like Alfonso. And she used to stop her ears up so as to be like Marie Thérèse. You should have seen her. It was very difficult to put up with.

— *Could it have been that she saw other people as incomplete, empty, and that she tried to fill and complete them with what she invented?*

— I see what you mean. But no, I think it was the opposite of that. I think she must have seen other people as impossible to know by the usual means — conversation, feeling. Like blocks, in fact. But I don't know how to explain it exactly.

That was the reason I first fell in love with her. I've thought about it a lot and I'm sure of it. And when I turned

55

away from her to other women, it was for the same reason:
she didn't need me. It was as if she could do without me,
didn't need to know me or understand me.

— *So what was it she was inhabited by? Say the first
word that comes into your head.*
— I don't know. I can't. Her?
— *Who do you mean?*
— I don't know.

— *Do you find talking about her boring or interesting?*
— Interesting.
More interesting than I would have thought.
Perhaps because it's all over.

Have they asked her that question?
— *I don't know. I don't think so.*
I believe she never wrote letters?
— I know she used to write to the papers at one time.
But I don't think she's done it for ten years now, perhaps
more. No. She must almost have forgotten how to write.
Besides, there was no one left in Cahors for her to write
to, except her uncle. He's her mother's youngest brother,
about the same age as she is. But she didn't ca_ɔ about
writing to him.
— *What about that man, the policeman in Cahors?*
— How do you know about him?
— *She mentioned him to the examining magistrate.*

— No, I don't think she wrote to him. No, not even at
the beginning, I don't think.
When you know her it's impossible to think of her sitting
down and writing to someone, telling them her news and
asking them for theirs. Just as impossible as trying to
imagine her reading a book. Of course when she wrote to
the papers she could just put down anything that came
into her head.

— *Didn't she ever see the policeman again after you were married?*
— As far as I know, no, never.
She'd been very unhappy with him. I think she wanted to forget him.
— *When?*
— When she met me, she wanted to forget him.
— *Was it to forget him that she got married?*
— I don't know.
— *Why did you marry her?*
— I fell in love with her. She was very attractive to me physically. I was mad about her in that way. That was probably what made me blind to all the rest.
— *The rest?*
— The strangeness of her character. Her madness.

— *Do you think you succeeded in making her forget the policeman in Cahors?*
— I don't think so. It was time that did it in the end, not me. And even if it was me, I didn't take his place.

— *Didn't she ever talk to you about him?*
— No, never. Though I knew she used to think about him, especially at first. But I knew that at the same time she wanted to forget him. When Marie-Thérèse came she didn't even bother to find out whether she'd known him in Cahors. I know that for sure.
It was because of him we never went to Cahors for our holidays. I didn't want her to see him again. I'd been told he'd tried to find out her address and I didn't want to take any risks.
— *So you didn't want to lose her?*
— No, in spite of everything. No, even after the beginning.
— *And you never spoke to her about the policeman in Cahors yourself?*

— No.

— *Had she asked you not to?*

— No. But there was no reason why I should. What was the point? Just to have her tell me she still loved him?

— *You're the sort of person who prefers not to talk about things that hurt you?*

— Yes, I am.

— *You knew that she'd tried to kill herself because of him? That she'd thrown herself into a pond?*

— I found out about it a couple of years after we were married.

— *How?*

— I belonged to a political party in those days. My memory of it is all mixed up with politics because the chap who told me was a friend in the same group who came from Cahors and happened to have heard about it by chance. But we didn't go in much for private conversations in the party, and we soon went on to talk about something else.

— *You didn't speak to her about it?*

— No.

— *And it didn't change your attitude towards her?*

— Yes, it did. How could I help feeling differently? I knew she wouldn't have killed herself if I'd left her.

— *Did you ever think of it?*

— Yes, but not seriously enough actually to do it.

— *Before you heard about it, would you have thought she was capable of suicide?*

— I wasn't all that surprised when I heard. So I suppose I must have thought she was capable of it. But this awful thing she's done now — of course I wouldn't have thought she was capable of that.

— *Are you sure?*

—

— *Why didn't you ever leave her?*

— The things I had to complain of weren't sufficient grounds for divorce. She didn't look after the house properly, but Marie-Thérèse soon came so that wasn't a problem any more.

These last few days I've been thinking over what our life was like. There was a time when I still loved her too much to leave her — that was when I suffered the most from her indifference. Then for years, after I'd begun to go with other women, her indifference charmed and attracted me instead of hurting me. She still had very winning moods sometimes. Then for a whole evening she'd be like a visitor. Until she was quite old she still had very charming manners, and a smile like a girl's.

Later on all that was completely finished.

— *You each kept your property separate when you married?*
— Yes. That was my idea.

— *Were you afraid of what she'd do if you left her?*
— No, not at all.
She'd probably have gone back to Cahors. Perhaps to the dairy. There wouldn't have been anything to be frightened of.
— *And there was never any question of a divorce?*
—No, I never mentioned it.
Perhaps I never met another woman I loved enough to leave her. I thought I had once or twice but now, looking back on it, I know I never loved anyone else as I loved her. She doesn't know that.

— *Did you know about the other man before you married her?*
— Yes, she'd told me. She didn't tell me they'd lived together. But I heard about it before we were married,

59

and also that she'd been very unhappy with him. I decided to let bygones be bygones. You can't prevent a woman of thirty from having a past. And besides, I wanted her to belong to me, I'd have overlooked anything.

— *Couldn't you have lived with her without marrying her?*

— I don't know, I never thought of it.

It's twenty-four years ago now. As if it were in another life.

— *When you look back over it all, do you regret having married her?*

— Oh, whether I regret it or not nothing matters any more.

— *But do you?*

— I regret everything I've done.

— *But her more than the rest?*

— No. I've had moments of happiness with her that I can't regret.

It's only her that interests you in all I tell you, isn't it?

— *Yes.*

— Just because of this murder?

— *Well, it's because of that I've come to be interested in her.*

— Because she's mad?

— *More because she's someone who's never come to terms with life.*

— Does what I tell you help you to find an explanation for what she did?

— *Several explanations, different from those I had before I spoke to you. But in the book I'm not allowed to decide on one.*

— That's just words. What's done can't be undone.

— *What you've just said: "Just words. What's done can't*

be undone" — those are expressions you often use, aren't they?

— Yes, I suppose so. I spoke from habit. Like the fool I am.

— *Why do you say that? You said it automatically, like what you said before.*

— Yes, I suppose I did.

— *I imagine she never speaks like that?*

— No. She never makes remarks about life.

— *Are there any other reasons why you didn't divorce her?*

— Well, there are so many who are worse off than me.

And then, to tell you the truth, with her I was free. She never asked me a single question. I'd never have had such freedom with anybody else. I know they aren't very brilliant reasons, but it's the truth. Now that it's all over I don't mind who knows it: I used to think that if I'd been unfaithful to her, that I loved so much, I'd have been even more unfaithful to the others, only it wouldn't have been nearly so easy. That's what I thought. I was disillusioned.

And then, as I told you, for a long time she was still attractive to me. You know what I mean — there was nothing I could do about it.

Once, in that political party, I met a young woman I'd have liked to live with. She was free and very attractive. She was younger than I was, but she didn't mind — especially as I didn't look my age in those days. We went together for two years.

Every so often I'd tell Claire I had to go away on business, but I was really with her. Once we went to the Côte d'Azur. For a fortnight. We went to Nice. It was agreed that after that I was to make up my mind either to leave Claire or break with the girl. I broke with the girl.

— *Why?*

— Perhaps it was because she was jealous of Claire and made use of everything I'd told her to try to persuade me to leave her.

Or perhaps I was too used to Claire, who's never made any demands on me. This is all over and above what I told you about being free and being fond of her.

— *Were you ever tempted . . . was there ever anything between you and Marie Thérèse Bousquet?*

— You could say it crossed my mind sometimes, but no more than that. I'm not a person that goes in for that kind of thing.

— *What kind of thing?*

— I mean someone who was employed in the house and was my wife's cousin into the bargain.

Marie-Thérèse herself wasn't one to make difficulties, as I suppose you've been told?

— *I've been told she was often seen in the forest in the evening with various Portuguese. But she never had a proper affaire with anyone?*

— No. How could she? Deaf and dumb like that.

— *What about Alfonso?*

— I don't think so but of course I can't swear to it.

— *If you were asked what role you'd played in the life of Claire Bousquet, what would you say?*

— I must admit I've never asked myself the question.

— *It's a fairly meaningless question. But you could try to give an answer.*

— I don't know what role I've played in her life. I don't see that I've played any.

— *What would have happened to her if you hadn't married her?*

— Oh, someone else would have married her. She was extremely charming. Her life would have been just the same. I'm sure of that. She would have taken the heart out of any man the same way as she took the heart out of me.

I expect other men would have left her, but she would have found others. I'm sure of that too.

You remember my saying she'd lied to me about certain things in her past?
— *Yes.*
— What I meant was that before we met she'd had lots of lovers.
— *Immediately after she'd tried to commit suicide?*
— Yes, for two years.
I didn't know anything about it. I only found out after we were married.
— *Did she actually lie to you? or just not say anything about it?*
— She just didn't say anything about it, though the normal thing would have been to have told me. And later on, when I asked her about it, she denied it. Why? Don't ask me.
— *So in fact you did talk to her about her past?*
— On that occasion, yes. It was a few weeks after we were married. We never talked about it again.
Now I'll answer your question. Anyone else but me . . . well, most people . . . would have thought that they'd saved her by marrying her. That that was the role, probably the only one, that they'd played in her life.
— *And didn't you ever think that?*
— In my bad moments, yes. That's what I used to say to the other women. But I knew it wasn't true. I knew very well you can't save someone who doesn't give a curse whether they're saved or not. What was I supposed to have saved her from? And what was I supposed to have given her instead? I haven't got anything against whores.
If no one had married her she would have gone on sleeping with Tom, Dick and Harry until she got old, and working her fingers to the bone in her dairy. So what?
Now I think she'd have been just as well off.

— Better?

— Oh, as far as she's concerned, she would have made do with that life the same as any other. Nothing would have changed her. And one day there would have been this awful thing. Whether she'd lived with me or with anyone else there'd have been a murder, I'm sure of it.

Even with the policeman in Cahors — I'm sure she had no idea of the life she'd have liked to live with him. I mean she hadn't fixed on one way of living rather than another.

— The people in Viorne — the tradespeople and the neighbours — say that as far as they know you never quarrelled.

— No, never. We didn't even do that.

What else do they say?

— They say, as you did, that you used to have affaires with other women, even women from Viorne. And that your wife knew and didn't mind.

She must have done some work in the house before Marie-Thérèse came?

— Yes, but just anyhow. She was good at cleaning. But she never learned how to cook.

— What did she do in the house after Marie-Thérèse came?

— Less and less every year.

— Yes, but what?

— She did the shopping every other day. She did her own bedroom. Nowhere else. She always did that, and very thoroughly. Too thoroughly.

She spent a long time getting dressed. At least an hour every morning.

For years she used to go out a lot, either in Viorne or to Paris. She used to go to Paris to the cinema. Or she'd go and watch Alfonso cutting wood. She watched television.

She washed her own things — she wouldn't let Marie-Thérèse do them.

Who can say what else she did? She'd be out in the garden, but doing what?

I didn't see much of her. On my days off I'd be working in the kitchen garden at the back — the proper garden's in the front. Marie-Thérèse would be in the kitchen or hanging round somewhere in Viorne. We used to meet at night at dinner. We'd have to call Claire about ten times before she'd come to the table.

But during these last years, and especially these last months, since the spring, she spent all her time outside, sitting on the bench doing nothing at all. I know it's difficult to believe, but it's true.

— *Marie-Thérèse was a good cook?*
— Excellent, if you ask me.
— *The best you've come across?*
— Yes. And I often used to eat out so I had standards of comparison. I always ate best at home.
— *Did your wife like her cousin's cooking?*
— Yes, I think so. She never said anything about it.
— *Nothing? Are you sure?*
— Yes. Why?
— *And didn't Marie-Thérèse ever take a holiday?*
— You mustn't get it wrong, she wasn't a servant. If she'd wanted to go away for a fortnight she could have done, she was quite free.
— *But she never went?*
— No. She was the real mistress of the house. It was her home. She made all the decisions — what we had to eat, the repairs that needed doing. For her, going away would have meant leaving her nice clean house to that slut of a Claire.
— *So for twenty-one years Claire, your wife, ate Marie-Thérèse Bousquet's cooking?*

65

— Yes. Why?

It was very good cooking, excellent, and very well planned and balanced.

— *And the two women never quarrelled either?*

— No. Of course I can't swear to it: I left them on their own together all day, and often, as I told you, I'd be away for a few days. But I don't think they quarrelled.

— *Think hard.*

— I am.

No, I can't remember anything.

— *How did she speak of her?*

— Just ordinarily. Once she called me and made me look at her from the door of the kitchen. She was laughing. She said: "Look, from behind she looks just like a little ox." We laughed, but not unkindly. It was quite true. Often when I saw Marie-Thérèse afterwards I'd remember it.

Sometimes, when they were younger, I used to come back in the evening and find them playing cards together. Especially in the winter. No, I think they got on quite well.

No quarrels. How could there have been? My wife never found fault with anything. And if there'd been the slightest upset between them, no matter how long ago, you can imagine it would have been the first thing I'd have told the magistrate.

— *It's very rare for people who live together to get on so well.*

— I know. It would have been better if we hadn't.

— *Do you really think that?*

— Yes. But it was impossible to pick a quarrel with Claire. If you pretended to be angry she saw through it and laughed.

— What could you have done?
— I don't know. I don't think about it. It's too late.

— So it was a very peaceful house?
— Yes. With the two women getting on so well together, perhaps I was lulled into a false sense of security. If I ever slept away from home I could never sleep properly — the people talked too loud and it didn't seem clean. I was used to them both. I feel as if I'd just woken up.

It was as if there was no one in the house. And yet everything was looked after — the cooking, the cleaning, everything.

— You said a little while ago that Marie-Thérèse kept an eye on Claire. In the nicest possible way, you said.
— Yes, especially lately. It was necessary. Claire sometimes did silly things, risky things. Marie-Thérèse used to tell me. When I was there I'd send Claire up to her room or out into the garden and we didn't say any more about it. It was best to leave her on her own.
— What about when you weren't there?
— Marie-Thérèse did it.
— But that didn't disturb the peace?
— No. It would have been more likely to disturb the peace if we'd just let her do as she liked.
— What, for instance?
— Well, she'd destroy things, or do things that might have been dangerous. She used to burn all the newspapers at once on the fire. She broke things, plates mostly, or threw them in the dustbin. Or hid things in corners or buried them in the garden: she said she'd lost her watch and her wedding-ring, but I'm sure they're in the garden. And she used to cut things up. Once I remember she cut every blanket on her bed up into three equal strips. But all you had to do was be careful not to leave matches or scissors lying about.

— *But what about when Marie-Thérèse was out?*

— When I wasn't there Marie-Thérèse never left her alone in the house. We kept the kitchen and our bedrooms locked, otherwise she would have been poking about everywhere. But once these precautions had been taken it was all right. I was telling you the truth when I said everything was peaceful and they got on very well. Claire didn't mind being sent out into the garden — she used to go straight away.

— *What would she have searched your rooms for?*

— Oh, that was really crazy. To find what she called "particular traces" that had to be got rid of. It was a complete mystery to me.

— *So you were most at ease when she was in the garden?*

— Yes, of course.

— *And everything was left unlocked at night?*

— I have a feeling that sometimes, especially lately, Marie-Thérèse used to lock the kitchen. I'm not sure. Perhaps she locked it because she was going to spend the night with one of her Portuguese.

— *Did she have them in her room sometimes?*

— Probably. Once I was up in my room I didn't bother about what was going on downstairs. Marie-Thérèse was quite entitled to entertain who she wanted when she wanted.

— *You didn't hear anything on the night of the murder?*

— No cries. I heard something that sounded like a door opening or shutting. I must have thought it was Marie-Thérèse coming in, or one or the other of them roaming round the house. I went back to sleep. My room was on the second floor. I could hardly hear any noise that was made on the ground floor.

— *You've left your house?*

— Yes. I've taken a room at the station hotel.

— *Have you been back to the Balto?*
— No, I use the hotel bar.
— *Why haven't you been back?*
— I want to make a break with my past. Even the good things in it. Even Robert Lamy.
— *What are you going to do? Have you thought about it?*
— Sell the house. Go and live somewhere else.

— *And Claire got on well with the tradespeople and the others in the village too, did she?*
— Yes. There was never any trouble there either. As I told you, Claire did the shopping every other day. But there was never anything.
— *Did she choose what she was going to buy?*
— No. Marie-Thérèse used to give her a list.
— *Robert and Alfonso were your best friends?*
— They were the people we liked best. She liked Alfonso best of all.

— *And in all these years you don't remember anything that might have foreshadowed the murder, even in the remotest way?*
— Nothing. I've racked my brains. But I can't think of anything.
— *And you never thought — even just once — that she was capable of doing what she's just done?*
— You asked me that before, when we were talking about suicide.
— *No, it was you who mentioned it then. Then I asked you if you were sure, and you didn't answer.*
— Well, I'll answer now. No, I'd never have imagined that she was capable of doing what she's just done. Never. If anyone had asked me I'd have laughed.
— *Think hard.*
— No, I don't want to. You can remember anything

if you try, or nothing, as you like. So I won't say anything.

— *She was indifferent, but not cruel, was that it?*
— On the contrary she was very tenderhearted as a girl.
I think she stayed like it.
— *You're not sure?*
— I didn't pay enough attention to be sure.
— *What were Marie-Thérèse's feelings about her?*
— She must have been very fond of her. But she concen-
trated on me more than her, Claire's not the sort of person
people lavish attention on. It's more likely to make her
awkward than to please her if you make a fuss of her.
And then of course Marie-Thérèse had a soft spot for
men, whoever they were. Anyone in Viorne will tell you
that.

— *And what do you think now? Do you think that no
matter what sort of life Claire had had it would have ended
in murder?*
— Well, this is what I think: the life she had with me
was a sort of average life, comparatively easy from the
material point of view and free, for better or worse, from
quarrels. So there's no reason why lots of the other lives
she might have had shouldn't have led her to the same result.
No, I can't think of any life for her that would have
avoided the murder.
— *What about with another man? In another place?*
— No. I think she would have done it anywhere, with
any man.

— *Has talking about her like this made you see any
things that could have been avoided?*
— Even if we'd remained the same to one another as we
were in the first few years, I don't think I'd have under-

stood any more. Of course I can only speak for myself. Someone more observant, more sensitive, might have realized she was heading for disaster. But I don't think he'd have been able to prevent it.

I could never guess what she was thinking, or what she was going to say or do.

Perhaps a minute before she killed her she didn't know she was going to kill her. Don't you think that's possible?
— *I don't know.*
She never asked you anything about the train intersections?
— No, of course not. Whatever people may say she must have thought of that trick at the last moment. After walking about Viorne all night with her bag she must have come to the viaduct just as a train was going by underneath, and it suddenly occurred to her how she could make use of it. I can see her as plainly as if I were there. I think the detective was right about that.
— *You haven't any idea about the head?*
— No, none. I looked in the garden, just on the off-chance, near the English mint. Nothing.
— *What's your opinion about the motives?*

— If you ask me it was just that she was mad. I think she's always been mad. No one had a chance to notice it because it only showed itself to her, when she was alone — especially in her room or in the garden. Terrible things must have gone through her mind there. I have a fair idea of the modern theories, and what I'd have liked would have been for you to talk to that policeman in Cahors. But he died last year.
— *Does she know?*
— I don't think so. I didn't tell her. And Marie-Thérèse didn't know anything about him. So I don't see who could have told her.

— I believe she spoke about him to the magistrate as if he was still alive.

Do you think he knew her better than anybody else?

— Perhaps. They'd known each other since they were children. He was the only one who could have said what she was like when she was twenty.

But who knows? I don't think she could have been very different when she was young from what she is now. I don't think she can have altered. Otherwise something of what she was like before would have been bound to survive.

When I come to think of it I don't think she's changed much since I first knew her. It's as if madness had kept her young.

— But if you hadn't been told about it, would you have imagined her having a passionate love affair? one that led her to suicide?

— No, that's true, I wouldn't.

But I don't think it was he that changed her.

— But how could she have had that passionate affaire if she'd always been like she was when you met her? — if she hadn't changed?

And how can you imagine her capable of such an experience if she wasn't different then from what she is now?

— She must have experienced it alone, for her part, as she did everything else. As she did with me. You mustn't run away with the idea that she didn't love me at all, you'd be wrong if you did.

Do you think it all started with that man?

— No, I don't. I agree with you.

Do you think she was unhappy?

— No. She wasn't unhappy. What do you think?

— I don't think she was unhappy either. That's not the point.

— You're right. That's not the point.

— *Apparently she's very talkative when she's questioned.*
— Who'd have thought it? But it's quite possible.
— *Did she always say very little, or did she sometimes go on chattering as if she couldn't stop?*
— Occasionally. The same as with everyone else. Just now and again. But to tell the truth when she went on like that we didn't listen.
— *What was it about?*
— Oh, anything. Imaginary conversations — I've told you about those. It never had anything to do with what we were interested in.
— *We?*
— Marie-Thérèse, me, the people in the bar.
— *What about Alfonso?*
— What she said did interest Alfonso a bit. She used to tell him about what she'd seen on television. We used to just leave them to get on with it.

As you probably know, we used to go to the Balto nearly every evening — until the murder. For the next five days I didn't go, I was too depressed. She didn't want to go either.

And then all of a sudden, after five days, at the end of the day, she came into the house to find me and told me she wanted to go to Robert's.
— *Was that the day the papers announced that the murder had been committed in Viorne?*
— The day after. I thought she was coming back to life a bit. Just as we were going she told me to go on. She said she had something to do and would join me. She wanted to pack that case, as you probably know.
— *Yes.*
— I might as well tell you that when she chucked the

73

transistor down the well I went to the doctor and asked him to come and see her. I didn't tell her I'd been. He was supposed to come this week. I'd made up my mind that the time had come for me to make a decision.

— *And she hardly said a word to you during those five days — between the murder and her confession on the evening of the 13th?*

— Hardly. She didn't even notice me walking across the garden when I came home.

I'd become as much a stranger to her as if I'd never known her.

— *She threw your glasses down the well too, didn't she?*

— Yes. Her own as well, and probably the key of the cellar. They haven't been able to find it.

— *Did she tell you?*

— No. I saw her from the dining-room as she threw the glasses down. But not the key.

— *Why do you think she threw away the glasses?*

— I did think it was to stop me from reading the paper and finding out there'd been a murder in Viorne. But now I think she had another reason.

— *So that the disaster should be complete?*

— So that it should be . . . sealed off is the phrase that occurs to me.

— *She told the magistrate she asked Alfonso to help her throw the television set down the well.*

— But you know that's not true?

— *Yes.*

— She'd dragged it into the hall and pushed it up against Marie-Thérèse's door and thrown an old black skirt of hers over it.

— *I know. But why do you think she said that about Alfonso?*

— Perhaps she meant to ask him to help her and thinks

74

she actually did, or perhaps she did ask him and naturally he refused. Otherwise I can't explain it.

What does Alfonso say?

— *He says she made it all up, she never asked him anything of the kind. But still Alfonso is the only person she could have asked to do something like that, isn't he?*

— Yes.

I can't make out how she had the strength to drag the set into the hall. I'd gone out to get some bread, and when I came back there it was.

— *Did you say anything to her about it?*

— No, I just put it back in its proper place. She didn't notice it that day. And the next day she was arrested.

— *When Alfonso says she made it all up it's possible he's lying?*

— Yes.

— *And Robert could have lied too?*

— No, only Alfonso. He has a sort of affection for Claire. You can tell by the way he smiles when he sees her.

— *Affection or love?*

— Oh, I don't know.

— *So if anyone could have guessed what she'd done it would have been he?*

— No one could have guessed. But if there was anyone in Viorne who could have guessed that she was heading for disaster it would have been Alfonso. If he'd been intelligent he would have understood her. He was probably closer to her than anyone. Even me... Yes. He was still very taken with her.

Does she know he's left the country?

— *I don't think so.*

Have you got any other explanation for the murder?

— It's very difficult to explain what I think.

I think that if Claire hadn't killed Marie-Thérèse she would have ended up killing someone else.

— *You?*

— Yes. She was moving towards murder in the dark, and it didn't matter who was at the end of the tunnel, Marie-Thérèse or me. . .

— *What was the difference between you and Marie-Thérèse?*

— I would have heard her coming.

— *Who ought she to have killed, according to the logic of her madness?*

— Me.

— *You just said Marie-Thérèse or you.*

— I've just realized the truth.

— *Why you?*

— Yes, it's inexplicable. I know.

— *You haven't any papers of hers, things in her own handwriting, even from a long time ago?*

— No, nothing.

— *We haven't got the least scrap of her handwriting. Didn't you ever find anything?*

— Two or three years ago I found some drafts of those letters she wrote to the papers in Versailles. They were hardly legible and full of spelling mistakes. I threw them on the fire.

— *What were they about?*

— I only glanced at them. I can only remember one. She was writing for advice about the garden, yes it was about the English mint, she wanted to know how to grow it indoors in winter. She kept making spelling mistakes.*

But she wrote something on the body?

* Tr.: In the French text Pierre specifies Claire's mistakes: instead of "*la menthe anglaise*" she put "*l'amante*" (feminine for "lover") and "*en glaise*" (made of clay or sand).

— Yes. Always the same two words. On the walls too. "Alfonso" on one wall. And "Cahors" on the other. That's all. No spelling mistakes.

— I haven't been down to the cellar since. I never shall. Alfonso. Cahors.

— Yes.

— So she still remembered the policeman in Cahors.

— Yes.

— What will they do to her?

— I don't know. Does it worry you?

— No, not really. Not now.

— Would she have confessed if you hadn't spoken as you did in the café? I wonder.

I don't think we shall ever know.

Apparently she really meant to go to Cahors. They found her toilet things in her case, and a nightdress — all the things she'd need for a journey. It's possible she really intended to go, and it was what you said that made her stay. Perhaps she stayed to correct the mistake you made when you said you thought the murder had been done in the forest.

— I can't tell you anything about that.

— You said: "I don't know what got into me."

— That's right.

— The papers had been talking about the murder for ten days. You'd known for three days that it had probably been committed in Viorne. The victim was a woman of the same age and build as Marie-Thérèse Bousquet. And according to Claire she'd chosen precisely this moment to go back to Cahors, where she hadn't been for years. . . . And yet you never had the least suspicion?

— No. Not the slightest inkling that there had been a murder in my house.

I think, indirectly, it must have been the situation I was

in that made me say those idiotic things about Alfonso and murder in general. The situation I was in since Marie-Thérèse had gone. That's the only connection I can see between what I said and the murder. The murder seemed to offer me the chance to throw the blame on someone for everything that happened in Viorne, including my troubles.

— *Who were you actually talking to in the Balto?*
— Everyone and no one.
— *Why did you single out Alfonso?*

— I suppose because he was the one the police were most likely to suspect. And then his way of talking as if he knew more about it than we did got on my nerves.
— *Perhaps his way of going on with Claire too?*
— No. No, that was all one to me.
— *The detective said you talked the way journalists write in the papers.*
— Possibly. I read the papers a lot.
— *Did her attitude that evening strike you as strange?*
— No, she never talks when there are strangers at Robert's. She confessed completely off her own bat. When the detective repeated what I'd just made up — about the murder having been done in the forest — first of all she just said it wasn't in the forest. She said that two or three times without saying anything else. And then she confessed everything.
— *What were the words she used?*
— She said: "It wasn't in the forest that I killed Marie-Thérèse Bousquet. It was in the cellar at four o'clock in the morning."
I shall remember those words until my dying day.
You think it was the mistake about the place that made her confess?
— *Yes. I think that if you hadn't said that she would just have gone to Cahors.*

78

— And if there hadn't been a word of truth in what the detective said from beginning to end?

— *I think she still would have gone. There would have been no reason for her to say anything. But your theories started off correct and then suddenly went astray, and she couldn't prevent herself from correcting the mistake. From reinstating the truth.*

— In short it's as if I'd given her away to the police, because of the word "forest"?

— *She would have been found out in any case, I think.*

— A little while ago I said I thought Marie-Thérèse had gone because she'd had enough of us. Do you remember?

— *Yes.*

— That wasn't quite the truth. What I really thought was that Marie-Thérèse had had enough of her, Claire. But not of me. I thought she'd had enough of looking after someone who didn't appreciate what she did. I did appreciate it.

— *How do you like it at the hotel?*

— Not bad.

You think I wanted all this to happen so that I could get rid of Claire, don't you?

— *Yes.*

— But who would have looked after me, who'd have done the cooking now that Marie-Thérèse was dead?

— *Someone else. You said so yourself.*

Isn't that what's going to happen? You're going to buy another house and find a maid?

— Yes.

I'd like you to tell me all you think. I'm prepared to believe anything, about other people and about myself.

— *I think you didn't only want to get rid of Claire—*

79

you wanted to get rid of Marie-Thérèse too. You wanted both of them to vanish out of your life so that you would be on your own again. I think you'd dreamed about the end of that world. In other words, about the beginning of another. But one that would be given to you without your having to do anything.

III

— *Claire Lannes, how long have you lived in Viorne?*
— Ever since I left Cahors — apart from two years in Paris.
— *Ever since you married Pierre Lannes.*
— That's right.
— *You haven't any children?*
— No.
— *You don't work?*
— No.

— *What was your last job?*
— Cleaner at the local school. Tidying up the class-rooms.

— *You have confessed to the murder of your cousin, Marie-Thérèse Bousquet.*
— Yes.
— *You also admitted that you had no accomplice.*
—
— *You did it all by yourself?*
— Yes.
— *You still say your husband knew nothing about what you'd done?*
— Nothing at all. I took the pieces away during the night while he was asleep. He never woke up. I don't know what you want.
— *To talk to you.*
— About the murder?
— *Yes.*
— I see.

— *We'll begin with those journeys to and fro at night between your house and the viaduct. Is that all right?*

— Yes.

— *Did you ever meet anyone?*

— I told the magistrate. Once I met Alfonso. He's a woodcutter who lives in Viorne.

— *I know.*

— He was sitting on a stone at the side of the road, smoking. We said good-evening.

— *What time was it?*

— Between two and half-past two in the morning, I think.

— *He didn't seem surprised? Didn't ask you what you were doing there at that hour?*

— No. He was there himself, wasn't he?

— *What do you think he was doing?*

— I don't know. Waiting for the sun to rise perhaps. Who can say? I don't know anything about it.

— *You don't think it strange that he didn't ask you any questions?*

— No.

— *Were you frightened when you saw him?*

— No. What I was doing frightened me so much I wasn't afraid of anything else. I nearly went mad with fear in the cellar.

Who are you, another examining magistrate?

— *No.*

— Do I have to answer you?

— *Why, does it bother you?*

— No, I'm quite willing to answer questions about the murder, and about myself.

— *You told the magistrate: "One day Marie-Thérèse*

was in the kitchen . . ." But you didn't finish the sentence.
I'd like you to finish it for me.

— It's got nothing to do with the murder. But I'll finish
it if you like.

. . . She was in the kitchen making a stew. She was tast-
ing the gravy. It was in the evening, I'd gone into the
kitchen, I was looking at her from behind, and I saw she
had a sort of mark on her neck, just there.

What are they going to do to me?

— *They don't know yet.*

Is that all you want to say about that evening?

— Oh, there's plenty more. When she was dead the
mark was still there on her neck. I remembered seeing it
before.

— *Why did you mention that evening to the magistrate?*

— Because he asked me for dates. I was trying to sort it
all out. I think there must have been several nights
between the two times I saw the mark.

— *Why didn't you finish the sentence when you were
talking to the magistrate?*

— Because it had nothing to do with the murder. I
realized that when I was in the middle of the sentence, so
I stopped.

— *When was it, about?*

— If I'd known when it was I wouldn't have mentioned
the mark.

The weather was still cold.

I know what I've done is impossible.

— *Hadn't you ever seen the mark before?*

— No. I only saw it then because she'd got a new hair-
style that left her neck uncovered.

— *Did the new hair-style make her face look different
too?*

— No, not her face.

— *Who was Marie-Thérèse Bousquet?*

— She was my cousin. She'd been deaf and dumb from birth. She had to be found something to do, and she liked working in the house. She was very strong. She was always happy.

Someone told me that because I'm a woman they'll only send me to prison for the rest of my days. Does that mean I'll spend the rest of my days, every one, in that one place?

— *Do you think it just or unjust that you should be shut up?*

— As you like. Just, I think. But a bit unjust too.

— *Why a bit unjust?*

— Because I say all they want me to say and it doesn't make any difference. As far as I can make out if I didn't say anything the result would be the same, they'd keep me in prison just the same.

— *Don't you think it's hard on your husband?*

— No, not really. He's still alive, isn't he? And anyway. . .

— *What?*

— I wasn't all that fond of Pierre Lannes.

— *Why did he arrange for Marie-Thérèse Bousquet to come?*

— To help in the house. And it didn't cost anything.

— *It wasn't to do the cooking?*

— No, when he first arranged for her to come he didn't know she could cook. It was because it didn't cost anything. It was only afterwards he started to pay her, I think.

— *You keep saying you've told the police everything, but that isn't quite true.*

— Are you questioning me to find out what I haven't told them?

— *No. Do you believe me?*

— Yes, all right. I've told them everything except about

If I did manage to arrange my thoughts, if I could make everything clear, what would they do to me?

— *That would depend on what your motives were.*

— I know that the more clearly murderers explain themselves the more they execute them.

What do you say to that?

— *I say in spite of that risk you want the whole truth to be known.*

— I suppose you're right.

I ought to tell you I've dreamed I was killing all the people I've ever lived with, including the policeman in Cahors, my first lover and the person I loved most in all my life. I dreamed it several times about each one. So sooner or later I was bound to do it in real life. Now it's done I know I was bound to do it in real life, some day.

— *Your husband says you hadn't any cause for ill-will against Marie-Thérèse Bousquet — she did her work well, her cooking especially was excellent, and she herself was clean and honest and generous and looked after both of you very well. He said he never knew of any quarrel between you in twenty-one years.*

— She was deaf and dumb. No one could have quarrelled with her.

— *But if she hadn't been, would you have had any complaints to make of her?*

— How should I know?

— *But you agree with your husband about her?*

— The house belonged to her. She did whatever she wanted. It would never have occurred to me to have an opinion about what she did.

— *And now she's not there any more?*

— I can see the difference. Dust everywhere.

— *You prefer it like that?*

— It's supposed to be better clean, isn't it?

— *But what do you really prefer?*

— Cleanliness took up a lot of room in that house. Too much.

— *You mean it took the place of something else?*

— Perhaps.

— *What? Say the first word that comes into your head.*

— Time?

— *Cleanliness usurped the place of time, you mean?*

— Yes.

— *What about the delicious cooking?*

— The cooking was worse than the cleanliness.

Now everything's neglected. The stove's cold. There's congealed grease all over the tables, and on top of the grease, dust. You can't see through the windows any more. Every time there's a ray of sunlight you can see all the dust and grease. There isn't a single thing left that's clean, not a glass. We've used up every piece of crockery in the sideboard.

— *You say "now". But you're not there any more.*

— I know what the house is like just the same.

— *Like a garret?*

— I don't understand.

— *I mean as dirty as a garret.*

— No, why a garret?

— *If it had gone on like that what would have happened in the end?*

— But it is going on like that, there's no one to look after it. It began while I was still there. A whole week without doing any washing-up.

— *What will happen if it goes on like that?*

— If it went on you wouldn't be able to see anything. Grass would sprout up between the bricks; eventually there wouldn't be room to stand. If it went on, it would stop being a house, if you ask me, and turn into a pigsty.

— *Or a garret?*

— No, I tell you. A pigsty. It had made a good start by the time I was arrested.

— *Didn't you do anything to prevent it?*

— I didn't do anything one way or the other. I just let it get on with it.

As for where it will end, we'll see.

— *Were you on holiday?*

— When?

— *Since the house started to get dirty?*

— I never took holidays. There wasn't any point. My time was my own, my husband's salary is quite generous, and I've got an income of my own from a house I own in Cahors. Didn't my husband tell you?

— *Yes.*

How do you find the prison food?

— Am I supposed to say whether I like it?

— *Yes.*

— It's all right.

— *Is it good?*

— It's all right.

Am I saying what you want me to say?

Yes.

— You can tell them from me that if they think they ought to keep me in prison for the rest of my life, well, come on, let them get on with it.

— *Don't you miss anything of the life you used to live?*

— If it goes on as it is now I'm quite comfortable here. All my family are gone now, you know — I'd be as well off here as anywhere else.

— *But don't you miss anything?*

— When from?

— *The last few years, for example.*

— Alfonso.

Alfonso and everything.

— *She was the last surviving member of your family?*

— Not quite. There's still her father, my mother's eighth brother, Alfred Bousquet. My mother's name was Adeline. All the Bousquets are dead except Alfred, Marie-Thérèse's father. He only had the one daughter, but he was unlucky, she was deaf and dumb, and his wife died of grief.

I don't count my husband as my family.

She really was my family. When I think of her I always see the same picture: she's playing on the pavement with a cat. They used to say she was very cheerful for someone who was deaf and dumb — more cheerful than a normal person.

— *You didn't think of her as a different sort of being from you, in spite of her infirmity?*

— Of course not, not when she was dead.

— *And when she was alive?*

— When she was alive, the difference was that she was very fat and slept like a log every night and ate a lot.

— *And that made more of a difference than her being deaf and dumb?*

— Yes, perhaps. When she ate and walked about, sometimes I could hardly bear it. I didn't tell the magistrate that.

— *Could you try to say why? Why you didn't tell the magistrate?*

— Because he would have misunderstood, he would have thought I hated her, and I didn't hate her. So as I wasn't sure I could explain it to him properly, I decided not to say anything about it. Perhaps you think I'm a liar because just now I said I'd told everything and now I'm telling you something I didn't tell. But you'd be wrong, because what I've just told you is just to do with my character, that's all. All I'm saying is that I'm the sort of person who can't bear other people eating and sleeping well. That's all. If it had been someone else and not her sleeping and eating like that it would have been just the same. So it wasn't just because it was her that I couldn't stand it. It was because I couldn't stand it in anyone. Sometimes I used to leave the table and go out into the garden so as to look at something else. Sometimes I was sick. Especially when there was stew. That's something that gives me the horrors. I don't know why. We often used to have it in Cahors when I was a little girl. My mother used to make it because it made the meat go farther.

— *Why did Marie-Thérèse make it if you didn't like it?*
— For the sake of making it, to give us something to eat, without thinking. And for my husband, who's very fond of it, he won't get any more of it now, will he, she made it for him, for herself, for me, for nothing.
— *Didn't she know you didn't like stew?*
— I never told them.
— *Couldn't they have guessed?*
— No. I ate it just the same as they did. If I didn't watch them eating it I could manage to eat it myself.
— *Why didn't you ever tell her you hated stew?*
— I don't know.
— *Think.*

— I didn't think "I don't like stew", so I couldn't say it.
— *So it's only now, talking to me, that you realize you could have told them?*
— Perhaps. I must have swallowed tons of the stuff. I don't understand it.
— *Why didn't you just leave it?*
— Because in a way I liked it. Yes. I didn't dislike eating that horrible greasy gravy. It gave me something to think about in the garden all day afterwards.

Have I told you how fond I was of the garden? I could sit out there without being disturbed. In the house I could never be sure she wouldn't suddenly be coming up to me and kissing me, that's something I ought to tell you too. She was very fat and the rooms are very small. I felt she was too fat for the house.

— *Did you tell her?*
— No, I didn't.
— *Why?*
— Because it was only me, it wasn't anything to do with anybody else that when I saw her in the house she seemed too fat. Outside it was different. It wasn't only her. The same applied to my husband. He's as thin as a rake, and for me he was too tall for the house and sometimes I used to go out into the garden so as not to see his head scraping the ceiling.

They didn't come bothering me in the garden.
There's a concrete bench, and a bed of English mint. It's my favourite plant.
I don't mind telling you I sometimes felt very clever sitting on that concrete bench. I'd grow quite intelligent sitting there quiet and still — I used to have some very intelligent thoughts.

— *How did you know?*
— One knows.

But now it's all over. Now I'm only the person you see in front of you.

— *And who were you in the garden?*
— The one that'll be left after I'm dead.

— *You said you ate the stew even though you didn't like it.*
— Yes, I've just said so.
— *Did you do a lot of things that you liked and disliked at the same time?*

— Some.

— *In what way did you like them?*
— I've told you that too. I could think about them afterwards in the garden.
— *In the same way every day?*
— No, never.
— *Did you use to think about some other house?*
— No, about the one that was there.
— *But without them inside it?*
— No, not without them inside it. They were there, just behind me, inside it, I couldn't think of it without them.

I tried to think of explanations, explanations they could never have thought of themselves, there just behind me.
— *Explanations of what?*
— Oh, lots of things.

I don't know what I've done with my life up to now. I loved the policeman in Cahors. That's all.

Whose business is it whether I go to prison or not?
— *No one's and everyone's.*
— I may look as if I'm worried about it, but really I don't care.

Did my husband tell you about the policeman in Cahors?
— *Not very much.*
— He doesn't know how much I loved him. You see me as I am now, but once I was twenty-five years old, and he was in love with me. He was marvellous. I believed in God then, and went to mass every day. I was in service in a dairy. He was living with another woman and because of that I wouldn't have anything to do with him at first. So he left her. We were madly in love with each other for two years. Madly. It was he who separated me from God. After God, I saw everything only through him. He was the only one I listened to, he was everything to me, and then one day I didn't have God any more, only him. And then one day he lied.

He was late. I was waiting for him. When he came in his eyes were shining, he talked and talked. I looked at him, I heard him saying he'd just come from the station, and what he'd been doing, all his lies, I looked at him, he talked faster and faster, and then suddenly he stopped. We just looked and looked at each other. The heavens fell.

I went back to the dairy. And three years later I met Pierre Lannes and he took me to Paris. I didn't have any children. I can't think what I've done with my life since.

— *Didn't you ever see the policeman from Cahors again?*

— Yes, once, in Paris. He came from Cahors to see me. He came to the flat while my husband was away. He took me to a hotel near the Gare de Lyon.

We cried together in the hotel room. He wanted me to go back to him but it was too late.

— *Why was it too late?*

— To love each other as we used to. We only knew how to cry. In the end there was nothing for it, I tore myself away from him, out of his arms, I had to pull his arms off me, he couldn't let me go. I got dressed in the dark and ran away. I ran away, and I got home just before my husband got back.

I don't think I thought about him so much after that. It was in that room near the Gare de Lyon that we left each other for ever.

— *Was Marie-Thérèse Bousquet already living with you when that happened?*

— No. She came the year after. My husband went to Cahors to fetch her. He brought her home on March 7, 1945, she was nineteen. It was a Sunday morning. I saw them coming up the Avenue de la République, I was in the garden. From a distance she looked just like everybody else. But close to, she didn't speak. But she understood by watching people's lips. You could never call her, you had to go up and touch her on the shoulder.

The house was very quiet, especially on winter evenings after the children had gone home from school. At seven o'clock you'd start to get the smell of cooking. She always used too much fat and the smell went all over the house, you couldn't get away from it.

In the winter I couldn't go out in the garden.

Have you asked the people in Viorne about the murder?

— Yes. And Robert Lamy.

— Thank God for him.

What did the others say?

— They said they couldn't understand it.

— I forgot to look at Viorne for the last time when I was in the police van. You don't think of these things. What I remember is the square at night, with Alfonso strolling up, smoking, and smiling at me.

— Some people say that you had all you needed to make you happy.

— My time was my own, my husband's pay is good, and I've got my own income from the house in Cahors — is that what they said?

— Yes. Others say they always expected it.

— Do they really?

— Are you unhappy now?

— No. I'm almost happy. I'm on the brink of being happy. If I had the garden I'd be over the brink and quite happy, but they'll never give it back to me, and now, now I prefer the sadness of being without it because I have to sleep with one eye open and be careful.

If I still had my garden it would be impossible, it would be too much.

What is it they say?
— *That you had all you needed to make you happy.*
— It's true.
I thought about happiness in the garden. I can't
remember anything at all of what I used to think sitting on
the bench. Now it's all over I can't make out what I used
to think.
Did Robert say I had all I needed to make me happy?
— *No. He said: "Things might have turned out differ-*
ently if Claire had had a different sort of life."
— What sort? Did he say?
— *No.*
— He might just as well have kept quiet then.
And Alfonso? What did he say?
— *I haven't spoken to Alfonso. But he hardly said any-*
thing to the magistrate. He didn't seem to have any very
clear ideas about you.
— He may not have said anything, but he must know
what to think about the murder.
— *Did he use to talk to you?*
— Of course not. What would we have had to say to
each other? But of course, having him there year in year
out, and saying good-morning and good-evening over and
over again for twenty-two years — it all adds up.
Apart from that we only spoke to each other sometimes
at night, in Viorne.
— *Why do you say: "Now it's all over"? Do you believe*
that?
— What could begin now? Well then, it's over.
Over for her that's dead. And over for me who did
it.
Over for the house. That lasted twenty-two years, but
now it's all over.
Just a single long, long day — day, night, day, night —
and then suddenly the murder.
I can remember the winter, when I couldn't go out in

the garden. Apart from that it's all the same. I believe I thought about everything, sitting on that bench.

I used to read the paper, and then afterwards, sitting on the bench, I used to think about what I'd read. About politics too, sometimes. Then people would go by and I used to think about them. I thought about Marie-Thérèse as well, about how she managed. I stopped my ears up with wax to see what it was like. Not often. About ten times perhaps, that's all. Did my husband say he was going to sell the house?

— *I don't know.*

— Oh, he'll sell it. The furniture too — what else can he do with it? He'll have it done by street-auction. The people of Viorne will all come and see the beds out there in the road. What do I care now what they think when they see the dust and the tables covered in grease and the dirty crockery. That's how it has to be.

He may have difficulty selling the house because of the murder having been done there. He may only get the price of the land. But I remember him saying building land in Viorne is worth about seven hundred francs a square metre now, so with the garden as well he shouldn't do so badly. What will he do with the money?

— *Do you think you had all you needed to make you happy?*

— From the point of view of the people who say that and believe it I suppose it's true. But for other people, looking at it from another point of view, no.

— *What other people?*

— You.

— *But you think I'm wrong too?*

— Yes. When you think of what it was like with the policeman in Cahors, you could say nothing exists beside that. But that's not true. I've never been separated from the happiness I had in Cahors, it overflowed on to all my life. You mustn't think it was just the happiness of a few years: it was a happiness to last for ever. It still goes on now, when I'm asleep — I see him smile at me over the hedge on his way back from work. I've always felt I'd like to tell someone about it, but who was there I could talk to about him? And now it's too late. Too far, too late.

I could have written letters about him, but who to?

— *To him?*

— No, he wouldn't have understood.

No, they ought to have been written to just anybody. But just anybody isn't easy to find. Still that's what I ought to have done: sent them to someone who didn't know either of us, so that it could all be completely understood.

— *To the papers perhaps?*

— No. I did write to the papers two or three times for various reasons, but never about anything so important.

— *What came between the garden and all the rest?*

— There was the moment when the smell of cooking started. You knew you had no more than an hour left till dinner, that you must think what you had to think quickly because there was only an hour left before the end of the day. Because that's what it was.

You see, monsieur, in the garden there was a sort of lid over my head, made of lead. My ideas would have had to get through the lid in order to ... well, for me to have some peace. But they hardly ever managed to get through. Mostly they just fell back again and stayed under the lid, swarming, and it hurt so much that several times I thought of doing away with myself so as not to have to suffer any more.

— *But sometimes they did get through the lid?*

— Sometimes, yes, they got out for a few days. I'm not mad, I know they never got anywhere. But when they

100

were going through me just to take flight, I was so ... the
happiness was so great I almost thought I had gone mad.
I thought people must be able to hear me thinking, that
my thoughts went off like gunshots in the street. The street
looked quite different. Sometimes people turned round
and looked at the garden as if someone had called them.
I mean that's what it seemed like.

— *What were these thoughts to do with? Your life?*
— If they'd been to do with my life they wouldn't have
made anyone turn round... No, they had to do with lots
of other things besides me and my surroundings. Others
might have taken them and made use of them. I had
thoughts about happiness, and plants in winter, certain
plants, certain things, food, politics, water, thoughts about
water, cold lakes, the beds of lakes, lakes on the beds
of lakes, about water, thirsty water that opens and swal-
lows up and closes again, lots of thoughts about water,
about creatures that crawl for ever without hands, about
what comes and goes, lots of thoughts about that too, about
the idea of Cahors when I think about it and the idea of it
when I don't, about television and how it's mixed up with
all the rest, one story upon another upon another, about
everything seething, a lot about that, seething and seething, and all it results in is more seething, about things
being mixed up and things being separate, oh, a lot about
that, seething that's separate and seething that's not, each
grain separate but stuck together too, seething multiplied
and divided, about the whole mess and all that's lost, and
so on and so on, ask me another.
— *About Alfonso too?*
— Yes, a lot, because he's utterly open-hearted, open-
handed, nothing in his house, nothing in his suit-case, and
no one to see that he's perfect.
— *Did you think about people who'd committed murder?*

— Yes, but I got it all wrong, I realize that now. But I couldn't talk about that except to someone else who'd done the same thing and could help me. Not to you.

— *Would you have liked other people to know about the thoughts you had in the garden?*

— Yes.

I'd have liked to let the others know that I'd got answers for them. But how? I wasn't intelligent enough for the intelligence that was in me, and I wouldn't have been able to express it. But take Pierre Lannes — he's too intelligent for the intelligence that's in him. I'd have liked to be altogether intelligent. The thing that consoles me for dying some day is not having been intelligent enough for the intelligence that's been in me all this time. I was never equal to it. I can see it must be awful to be very intelligent and to know that your intelligence must die just the same as you. But still I wish I'd been like that.

— *When did all this start?*

— In the empty classrooms, when I was doing the cleaning. It would still be warm from the children, and I'd be there alone with the figures on the blackboard, divisions and multiplications, multiplications and divisions, and I'd turn into the figure three, and it seemed quite true.

— *Your husband says that sometimes you thought you'd had conversations with people in the street.*

— Ah, he told you that, did he? I used to invent conversations when I felt like it. I knew very well neither of them believed me. I liked them to think I was mad occasionally, it put the wind up them, and then they'd give me a bit more peace.

But sometimes the conversations had really happened. Only not as I told them, never as I told them.

— *Let's get back to the murder, if you don't mind.*

— I know practically nothing about what happened then. They must have told you.

— *Why did you do it?*
— What are you referring to?
— *Why did you kill her?*
— If I could explain that all the interrogating would be over and you wouldn't be sitting here asking me questions. I know about the rest.
— *The rest?*

Yes. If I cut her up in pieces and threw the pieces on to the train it was because it was a way of getting rid of the body. Put yourself in my place. What would you have done?

Anyway, they say it wasn't such a bad idea.

I didn't want to get caught before I had to, and I got rid of her like someone with their head screwed on.

You can't imagine how tiring it was, all that butchery at night in the cellar. I'd never have believed it. If anyone tells you I added one crime to another in doing what I did in the cellar, you tell them it's not true.

You don't know why you killed her?
— I wouldn't say that.
— *What would you say?*
— That depends on the question I'm asked.
— *And you've never been asked the right question?*
— No. I'm telling the truth. If I'd been asked the right question I'd have found an answer. But I can't find the question any more than anyone else.
— *Do you think someone else could answer the question, why did you kill her?*
— No, no one. Except perhaps at the end.
— *And you don't try yourself to find out what the right question is?*
— Yes, but I haven't been able to. But I don't try very

hard. I had too much trouble doing it to be able to think about it.

They've fired question after question at me, and I haven't recognized one.

— *Not one?* ...

— No. They ask: Did she get on your nerves because she was deaf and dumb? or, Were you jealous of your husband? or of her being younger than you? Or, Were you unhappy, or, Was the running of the house a burden to you? At least you haven't asked me anything like that.

— *What's wrong with those questions?*

— They're separate.

— *And the right question would include all those and others as well?*

— Perhaps. How should I know? But you'd be interested to know why I did it?

— *Yes. I'm interested in you. So everything you do interests me.*

— Yes, but if I hadn't done this murder I wouldn't interest you at all. I'd still be sitting there like a clam in my garden. Sometimes my mouth felt like the concrete the bench was made of.

— *What would you consider a good question? I don't mean a question I might ask you, of course. One that you might ask me.*

— Why should I do that?

— *Well, to find out why I'm asking you questions, for example. In what way you interest me. What I'm like.*

— I know in what way I interest you. And I already know a bit what you're like.

As for the rest, I'll tell you what I used to do with Alfonso. When he called to talk to Pierre about work or anything, I used to stand in the corridor or behind the door and listen. It would need to be the same with you.

— *I'd have to be talking somewhere at a distance?*
— Yes, to someone else.
— *Without knowing you were listening?*
— That's right. It would have to happen like that, by chance.
— *Things can be understood better from behind a door?*
— Everything can. It's wonderful. Like that I've seen right into Alfonso, deeper even than he himself.
Whenever Pierre found me behind the door he used to tell me to go back into the garden, and quick. What a life.
— *What did Pierre's voice sound like through the door?*
— The same as ever.
Listen, I can't say fairer than this: if you find the right question, I swear I'll answer it for you.
What do they say were my motives for killing her?
— *People just make suppositions.*
— Like the magistrate, with his questions.
— *Is it better just to say "why"?*
— "Why"? Yes. There's no need to go any farther than that.
— *Well then, why?*

— True. Why.
But the word draws me towards you, towards the questions.
— *Supposing there was a motive, a reason, but one that's unknown?*
— Unknown to whom?
— *Everyone. You. Me.*
— And where is this unknown reason?
— *In you?*
— Why in me? Why not in her, or in the house, or in the knife? Or in death? Yes, in death.

Is madness a reason?

— *Perhaps.*

— When they get tired of looking and not finding anything, they'll say it's madness. I know.

Oh well. If it's madness I've got, if that's my illness, I'm not sorry.

— *Don't think about that.*

— I don't. It's you who think about it. I know when people think I'm mad. I can tell by the sound of their voices.

— *What did you use to do in the house?*

— Nothing. The shopping every other day. That's all.

— *But you must have done something to occupy yourself.*

— No.

— *But how did you pass the time?*

— It rushed by, at fifty miles an hour, like a torrent.

— *Your husband said you did your room every day.*

— Just for myself, I used to do my room and wash, wash my clothes and myself. Like that, you see, I was always ready, and so was the room. All clean and with my hair done and the bed made. Then I could go out into the garden without leaving a trace behind me.

Yes, in spite of what I said I am a bit sad that I'm mad. If the other women there are mad, what will become of me?

— *When your room was done and you were washed, what was it you were ready for?*

— Nothing. I was just ready. If things had to happen, I was ready, that's all. If someone had come for me, if I'd disappeared, if I'd never come back, ever, they'd have found I'd left nothing behind me, not a single trace that was particular, only traces pure and simple. That's all.

— *What are you thinking about?*

— The garden. Far away. Peaceful. Over. And there's Alfonso going on cutting wood, and all the time it's over. And Pierre going to the office. I think Alfonso had all that was needed to be intelligent too, but he wasn't, I shall never know why any more than I do about myself. There were two of us in Viorne in the same boat, Alfonso and me.

I don't think that about Pierre.

Do you think all I'm telling you is the truth?

— *I believe it's the truth.*

— There, you see. I believe it's the truth too. I've never talked so much and I'm telling the truth. Perhaps I could have done it before if the opportunity had presented itself.

I might never stop, I might go on talking for a year. Or I might stop straight away, one turn of the lock and finished for ever. It's like that now — I'm talking to you and not talking to you at the same time. Head still stuffed as full as ever. Always something inside there. What can you do — it's strange to be as we are. Have I told you about the house?

There were two bedrooms on the first floor and on the ground floor there was the dining-room and Marie-Thérèse's room.

— *Had you been asleep before you went down to her room?*

— I didn't have to switch the light on so it couldn't have still been dark. So I must have slept.

I often used to wake up at dawn and not be able to get to sleep again. Then I used to walk about the house, always downstairs.

The sun was coming in between the dining-room and the hall.

— *... The door of her room was open and you saw her asleep on her side with her back to you.*

— Yes. It was always like that.

107

—You went into the kitchen for a glass of water. You looked round you.

—Yes. On the underneath of the plates I can see what was written on the ones we bought in Cahors three days before we were married. "Bazar de l'Etoile 1942." It's starting all over again. I know I shall be drawn into thinking about the plates, about all that. And then I feel I've had enough. I want them to come and take me away. I want just three or four walls, a steel door, an iron bedstead, and a barred window, and Claire Lannes shut up inside. So I open the window and smash the plates so that they'll hear me and come and get rid of me. But suddenly she's standing there in the draught from the door. She watches me smashing the plates, and smiles, and goes to tell Pierre. She used to go and tell Pierre everything, and then Pierre would come, and quick march, out in the garden.
In the end I got to like the garden.

—When was this?
—When I broke the plates? That was three, five years ago.
—How could your husband have believed you when you said Marie-Thérèse had gone to Cahors?
—Oh, leave me alone for a minute.

What is it you want to know?
—What did you tell your husband when he got up?
—I said what you just said.
—Did your husband tell the truth?
—He didn't believe me. Nobody asked me about her, not even Alfonso.
—Didn't your husband ask any questions?
—No. That proves he didn't believe me. It's not true that he believed me.
—What did he believe then?

— What good would it do you to know that? I don't know.

— *And do you think Alfonso guessed?*

— Yes. When I asked him to throw the television down the well I saw he'd guessed.

What does he say?

— *He says you never asked him to throw the television down the well.*

— I don't believe you. Either they're all lying or you are.

— *Perhaps I've got mixed up.*

— Yes. Alfonso may not talk much, but he can say yes and no. Perhaps one day it'll come to him all of a sudden, like me. Sometimes he sings *La Traviata* on his way home. One day I asked him to. Apart from that he cuts wood all the time. How boring. A long time ago, twelve years, I hoped he might love me, Alfonso, and take me to live with him in the forest, but that love will never happen. Once I waited for him all night, I listened for every sound, I'd have known love again, Cahors again, together, but he didn't come.

They'll all say I'm mad now, in the way they'd be, if they were. They can say what they like, they're on the other side, they'll say anything, without thinking.

If they knew what happened in the cellar. If they'd been in the cellar for a single minute they'd soon shut up. They wouldn't be able to say a word about it all.

— *Were you on the same side as they are before the murder?*

— No, never, I've never been on their side. If I ever had to mix with them, say when I did the shopping — and I did the shopping every other day, don't go thinking I didn't do anything any more — well, then I had to say good-morning and all that, but I never said more than I had to. I'd still hear their voices rasping in my head an hour afterwards. Like actors in a theatre.

— Did you go to the theatre?
— Sometimes he took me when we lived in Paris.
La Traviata was in Cahors, with the other.
— But Alfonso wasn't on the other side?
— No, Alfonso was on my side, even if he didn't know it.
So was the policeman in Cahors. Both feet.
— Do you know what became of him?
— He's still in Cahors, shut up there leading the life he
likes, all over the place.

— Was your husband "on the other side"?
— Yes and no. I think he was cut out to be on the other
side, but because of us he never quite went over. If it
hadn't been for us he'd have invited them for meals, I'm
sure, and talked just like them. Good-morning, madame,
how are you? How are the children, getting taller every
day? An oak in every acorn. Sometimes he used to go to
see them. But he'd always come home to his nice warm
house reeking with grease — always, even after he'd spent
several days with the others, he'd still come back to us. Of
course there was never any question of our inviting them.
He knew he couldn't have them to his place with a wife
like me on one side and a deaf and dumb cousin on the
other. He was stuck. He knew that quite well. When you
get right down to it, he was on the other side too. . .
Yes but of course, with us two he'd got used to women
prowling round the house without saying a word and sitting in the garden without a sound.
Once, when I came back from a hotel near the Gare de
Lyon where I'd met the policeman from Cahors for the
last time, and I'd rushed back so that he shouldn't suspect,
I saw him come in with his tie and his glasses as if nothing
on earth were the matter, and there I was still crying, I
couldn't stop, the hot tears fell in spite of me, and that
day, when I saw him come in with his tie and his glasses
and his white collar, and that expression that seemed to say

110

"Go somewhere else and cry if you must, my girl", that day I realized already that he belonged on the other side. Already.

— *Did Marie-Thérèse Bousquet belong "on the other side"?*
— No, because of being deaf and dumb. But if she'd been normal she'd have been the queen of the other side. Mark my words — the queen. She used to devour them with her eyes as they went along the street to mass. They used to smile at her, which proves it. They always took good care not to smile at me.

She was deaf and dumb, a great lump of deaf meat, but sometimes little cries used to come out of her, not from the throat, from the chest.

I put on dark glasses in the cellar and switched the light out, so I wasn't mad, because I didn't want to see her and I did what was necessary so as not to see her, I switched off the light and put on the glasses. I'd seen enough of her to last me a century.
Did you hear what I just said? I'm talking differently now. I'm not separating my sentences. I've just noticed myself.
Does it bother you?
— *No.*
— I keep saying vulgar things and skipping from one subject to another. Don't think I don't know when I do it.
I'll stop talking for good. That's what I'll do.

— *On one wall of the cellar they found the name Alfonso written up with a piece of coal. Do you remember writing it?*
— No. Perhaps I wanted to call him to come and help

111

me? And because I couldn't shout, for fear of waking my husband, I wrote it? Perhaps. I don't remember.

I've written before to call for help when I knew all the time it wasn't any good.

— *Who to?*

— Oh, a man who didn't come back.

Marie-Thérèse used to do it, perhaps I caught it from her.

— *On the other wall there was the word "Cahors"*

— It's quite possible. I don't remember. I did so many things in that cellar.

Tell me, how is it possible?

— *Is it that you can't speak of the cellar or that you don't want to?*

— I don't want to.

I can't.

Besides, the cellar doesn't explain anything. I was just trying desperately to get rid of all that butchery. That's all it was, just desperate attempts, but enough to kill you, enough to make you howl. I must have fainted — once I came to and found I'd been asleep on the floor, and then I was sure. I can't, I won't. I'll die with my memories of the cellar. I'll take what happened there down with me into my grave. If everyone's revolted by me and all Viorne spits on me, it'll always serve to counterbalance the cellar.

— *The inhabitants of Viorne seem to be more important to you than you admit.*

— It's the background, Viorne. That's where I've lived the longest, in the middle of Viorne, right in the middle, knowing everything, day after day. Then one fine day, the murder. I can guess what they think, it's so easy, as clear as daylight. There's the murder, and if I shut my eyes I can see them poking their heads out of the window or standing at the door and saying in their actors' voices: "Yes, but I do think she went a bit too far."

112

— *You intended to go to Cahors?*

— Yes, on my word. I talk to you because you don't know anything and you really want to learn all there is to know. Whereas my husband thought he knew it all, it was a waste of time to talk to him. Yes, I meant to go to Cahors. I thought to myself that between the time they found out the murder was done in Viorne and the time they found out it was me who'd done it, I'd be able to go to Cahors for a few days.

I'd have gone to the Hotel Crystal.

— *Why didn't you go?*

— You know that — why do you ask me?

— *Because of what your husband said about the murder?*

— He was so ridiculous and he didn't realize it.

— *Is there another reason too?*

— Yes, I think so.

I was interested and I forgot the time.

It was the first time he'd talked about her so accurately.

Is that it?

— *It was her he was talking about?*

— Yes. He even said her name: Marie-Thérèse Bousquet.

So practically nothing more was needed for the whole truth about the murder to be known in a flash. Just one thing was needed, and I was the only person who knew what it was. As you know, when that happens you can't help telling them.

— *What was it you told them?*

— I whispered to Alfonso and it was he who told them. It was all quite simple. I said to Alfonso: "Tell them it was me, and that I want you to tell them." And then Alfonso went into the middle of the café and said: "You needn't look any further. It was Claire who stabbed her cousin while she was asleep and then disposed of the body in the

113

way we all know about." At first everyone was silent. Then people shouted.

Then the man took me away.

— *Alfonso says he met you sometimes at night in Viorne, too.*

— That's another matter. If he hadn't been out himself he wouldn't have met me.

Funny he should have said that.

— *I assure you he didn't mean any harm.*

— I know. If I walked about Viorne at night it was because it seemed to me there were things going on there that I ought to go and find out about.

I thought they were beating people to death in cellars. One night fires started to break out everywhere, but fortunately it rained and put them out.

— *Who was beating whom?*

— The police were beating foreigners in the cellars, foreigners or other people. They went away when it got light.

— *Did you see them?*

— No. As soon as I came it stopped.

But often I was mistaken and everything was quiet, quite quiet and peaceful.

What was I just saying?

— *You were talking about Alfonso.*

— Ah yes, Alfonso.

Will he go to prison too?

— *No.*

— I should have thought he would. So he goes on just as before? Living in the forest?

— *I don't know. Would you have liked him to go to prison?*

— Well, if I'm there I don't see why he shouldn't be there too. He knew everything from the beginning. But they haven't arrested him.

Still of course we wouldn't have been in the same prison, so it doesn't really make any difference.

— *What would you have done in Cahors?*
— I would have started something again for a few days. I'd have walked and walked through the streets. I'd have contemplated Cahors.
— *And would you have tried to find the policeman from Cahors?*
— Perhaps not. What would be the point, now? Then they would have come for me.

— *About the head. . .*
— Don't start again about the head. . .
— *I'm not asking you where it is. I just want to know in what way it was a problem to you.*
— To know what to do with it, where to put it.
— *But why the head especially?*
— Because it was the head. You can't just throw a head on to a train.

And the basket, what was I to do with that?

I had a proper funeral for her. I said the prayers for the dead. That was all I could think of, in spite of the fact that the policeman from Cahors separated me from God and I never found him again.

There, you see — I've ended up saying something about it and I didn't mean to.
— *And it was at that moment during the murder that you realized you'd killed her?*
— You guessed?

Yes, it was then. Do you believe me?
— *Yes.*
— First of all there was the mark on her neck — when I saw the mark she started to come back a bit from the dead. Then when I saw the head she came right back.

They ought to cut my head off too for what I've done.

An eye for an eye. That's what I'd do if I were them. I miss the garden. There's no grass in the prison yard. To punish us. A good idea. Nothing will ever take the place of my garden.

My husband ought to have been more careful. Sometimes I feel mad.

It was a ridiculous life.

— *You feel mad?*

— Yes, at night. I hear things. I think they're beating people. Sometimes I've thought so.

— *But if you didn't talk to your husband about it how was he to guess?*

— If I had talked to him about it he'd have put me in the asylum — I know him. Very neat and tidy in his ideas. A place for everything and everything in its place, that's his motto. You see?

Listen. The night of the murder she was crying out like I told you and I thought it was because of her I couldn't sleep. I wondered whether Alfonso mightn't be down there making love to her. He still needs women, you see. I'm older than he is. There's always been that difference of age between us, and it hasn't got any smaller. So I wondered whether he mightn't have fallen back on Marie-Thérèse. She's my cousin, my flesh and blood. The surname was the same, Cahors was there behind us both, we ate the same food under the same roof, and she was deaf and dumb.

I went downstairs. Alfonso wasn't there.

Now I won't say any more.

I knew Alfonso wasn't there. It was usually at his place, on Saturday afternoon, never anywhere else, and never at night. And so?

116

Do you know that murder doesn't happen all of a sudden? No. It creeps up slowly, like a tank. And then it stops. And there it is. A murder has just been committed in Viorne. By Claire Lannes. There's no going back on it. Murder has descended on Viorne. It was hovering high in the air above, and it's there where Viorne is that it fell, in that house, in the kitchen of that house, and the one who did it — oh . . . the one that did it is Claire Lannes. She knew that the murder was there, and that only a thread kept it from falling on Viorne.

So there you are, monsieur. I know some people can't bear to hear the name of Claire Lannes mentioned and prefer not to read the papers, but they're wrong. How was it possible to carry a body weighing fourteen stone as far as the train? How can you cut through a bone without a saw? They say there was blood in the cellar. But how can we prevent there being blood, you and I?

If they search the house, don't forget to tell them that the doors have always sloped to one side as you come down the stairs.

I'd be interested to know whether it's always the same with everyone who's done what I did.

— *Yes.*

— So that's not an explanation?

— *No.*

— In that case I can't see any way out. Ah well. I'm tired now. But it's a restful tiredness. Perhaps I'm very close to being mad. Or dead. Or alive. Who knows?

— *Let's talk about the book your husband made you read aloud every evening. Do you remember?*

— Yes. It was years ago. My husband thought I hadn't had enough education. He made me read a geography book. But he lost heart. I couldn't understand.

Is that all about the book?

117

— What was it you couldn't understand?

— I couldn't understand why he wanted me to know the geography of all the countries. Every day another country to learn, one a day, there was no end to it. He made me read so that I should have to be there near him, and to punish me for thinking about the policeman in Cahors. But I have remembered some of the things I read then: the famine in India, Tibet, and the town in Mexico that's a hundred and fifty feet up.

Is that all about the book?

— Yes. What about the comics you used to take out of the desks at school — do you remember anything about them?

— Hardly anything.

Did I tell you about where I put the head?

— No.

— Good. I must keep that secret. It's the only secret I've got left — I talk too much.

No one ever asked me questions. My road led straight to the murder. All my secrets are scattered to the winds. I feel like hiding my face. If I was in the garden, if you let me go, the people of Viorne would come and watch me and spy on me, and I'd have to go away. But where? You'll have to keep me. As for the garden, ah well, I'll have the memory.

I'm in with the common law prisoners. The other women say: "Have you seen the old girl from Viorne?" and laugh about the intersections. They ask me to explain about it, and I do.

A lawyer came to see me and told me I'd be going somewhere else, to a place where I'd forget what's happened. I didn't believe him.

The other women say I'm not really responsible. I hear them talking among themselves. But what do they know about it? I've been behaving very well. They've said so. I refused to see my husband a second time.

118

I know Alfonso won't come to see me... I shall die without seeing any of them again, all three. Ah well.

My life was lingering on too long and getting nowhere, and at first it was so beautiful with the policeman in Cahors. Ah well.

Aren't you going to say anything?

They gave me a pen and some paper. They told me to write whatever came into my head. Doesn't that interest you?

I tried, but I couldn't write a single word.

And yet I wrote to the papers before, oh, often — long letters too. Did I tell you? I don't suppose they ever got there.

— *In one of them you asked how to grow English mint in winter.*

— Did I? I used to eat it sometimes as a laxative. Perhaps I wrote to ask how to keep it green, so green. Perhaps. I don't remember. I wrote a lot of letters. Fifty-three. Or was it twelve. How I wish, oh how I wish I could explain.

My head used to seethe worse than a sewer before the murder. Now less and less.

The catch about the intersections makes them laugh. I didn't know you could do that. I was sure I'd never be found out.

I didn't think of the viaduct beforehand, I was going towards the river when I walked over it.

Then I thought to myself, never, never, with the head safely buried away, and with all the things they're always finding on trains, heaven knows what, I'll never be found out. But I was wrong. I saw a map of the intersections in the paper: Viorne is in the middle and all the trains pass through there, even those that are going a long way away.

119

They all have to go through Viorne. Did you know that?
It's the biggest junction in France. I lived there and I
didn't know. I picked on the wrong viaduct.

But all the others would have been too far away, walking and at night. So?

They found everything except the head — counted it
all, put it all together, every bit.

I'd never have believed it possible.

You don't say anything.
— *Now you must tell me where the head is.*

— Was it to get to that question that you asked me all
the others?
— *No.*

— If it was the magistrate who asked you to ask me
that, all you have to do is say I didn't answer.

What would you say if I said they're going to put me in
the mental hospital at Versailles?
— *I'd say you're right.*
Well, I've answered you.
— So I am mad then? What would you say if I asked
you if I'm mad?
— *I'd say "yes" again.*
— So you're talking to a madwoman?
— *Yes.*

— But what a madwoman says doesn't count. So why
ask me where the head is? Perhaps I don't remember
where I put it? Perhaps I've forgotten the exact spot?
— *Just a vague indication would be enough. Just a*
word. Forest. Bank.
— But why?
— *Curiosity.*

— You mean to say that only that one word counts among all the others? And you think I'm going to let you get it out of me? So that all the others can be buried alive, and me with them, in the asylum?

Oh no. You're going to have to spend a lot of time with me, you and others, before that word crosses my lips.
Do you hear?
— Yes.
— There are things I haven't told you. Do you want to know what they are?
— No.
— All right.

If I told you where the head is would you go on talking to me?
— No.

— I see you've lost heart.
— Yes.

— If I had managed to tell you why I killed that big fat deaf woman, would you go on talking to me?
— No, I don't think so.

— Do you want us to go on trying? Did I tell you she always called Pierre for everything? But she and I never quarrelled — did I tell you that? Never. And can you guess why? Because I was afraid they'd put me in the asylum before it was time.

What was it I said that suddenly made you lose heart?

It's late perhaps. Perhaps time is up?
It always happens the same way, whether you've committed a murder or nothing at all.

You seemed to like those children's comics. It was lovely but it was against the law. Fortunately Pierre told me.

— *What did he tell you?*

— Ah, you're waking up again. I don't remember what he said. That it was against the law.

— *What?*

— Stealing them from the desks. Not reading them. It was him who forbade Marie-Thérèse and me to read them.

Sometimes I used to look after the cloakroom at municipal dinners, did I tell you?

On the ground floor, when you came down the stairs, there were three doors, the first into the dining-room, the second on to the hall, and the third leading into her bedroom, they were always open, all three in a row on the same side, they all tilted the same way, it was as if the whole house sloped in that direction and she'd rolled right down to the bottom past the doors, you really needed to hold on to the banisters.

If I were you, I'd listen. Listen.

PANTHEON MODERN WRITERS ORIGINALS

THE VICE-CONSUL
by Marguerite Duras, translated from the French by Eileen Ellenbogen

The first American edition ever of the novel Marguerite Duras considers her best—a tale of passion and desperation set in India and Southeast Asia.

"A masterful novel." —*Chicago Tribune*

0-394-55898-7 cloth, $10.95   0-394-75026-8 paper, $6.95

MAPS
by Nuruddin Farah

The unforgettable story of one man's coming of age in the turmoil of modern Africa.

"A true and rich work of art. . . . [by] one of the finest contemporary African writers."
—Salman Rushdie

0-394-56325-5 cloth, $11.95   0-394-75548-0 paper, $7.95

DREAMING JUNGLES
by Michel Rio, translated from the French by William Carlson

A brilliant, hypnotic novel about an elegant French scientist who sets off to study chimpanzees in turn-of-the-century Africa, and his shattering confrontation with the jungle, passion, and at last, himself.

"Very beautiful and very witty." —Mark Strand

0-394-55661-5 cloth, $10.95   0-394-75035-7 paper, $6.95

BURNING PATIENCE
by Antonio Skármeta, translated from the Spanish by Katherine Silver

A charming story about the friendship that develops between Pablo Neruda, Latin America's greatest poet, and the postman who stops to receive his advice about love.

"The mix of the fictional and the real is masterful, and . . . gives the book its special appeal and brilliance." —*Christian Science Monitor*

0-394-55576-7 cloth, $10.95   0-394-75033-0 paper, $6.95

YOU CAN'T GET LOST IN CAPE TOWN
by Zoë Wicomb

Nine short stories powerfully evoke a young black woman's upbringing in South Africa.

"A superb first collection." —*The New York Times Book Review*

0-394-56030-2 cloth, $10.95   0-394-75309-7 paper, $6.95